Alex stirred restlessly in the bed, gradually becoming aware of something hard and lumpy

She squirmed again, trying to get comfortable. Failing. Something was digging painfully into her back. Feeling like the princess with the pea, she reached for the offending object. A pager. What was a pager doing in her bed?

No, not her bed. Kane's bed.

Coming fully awake, Alex gasped and sat upright. Memories of the night before flooded her mind. She'd never known any night could be that perfect, that beautiful.

That terrifying.

"Stay with me. Not just for tonight. Don't go back to Chicago."

The recollection of Kane's words had her dressed and fleeing out the door. She needed time to think. Time to try to convince herself that she hadn't really fallen helplessly, desperately in love with Kane.

Dr. Kane Lovell. There was no way she could pass the test as s̶

Dear Reader,

Many of you have written to tell me how much you've been enjoying the heroes in Temptation's **Rebels & Rogues** mini-series. Now you can discover magic and fantasy in **Lovers & Legends** from Temptation.

Through 1994 we shall be bringing you some of the most enduring and appealing fairy tales and legends retold in sizzling Temptation style!

This month we bring you ever-popular Gina Wilkins's modern-day version of *The Princess and the Pea* — a light-hearted, spirited rendition of the "tests" our fair heroine must pass before she can win the hand and heart of her prince.

I hope you enjoy the magic of **Lovers & Legends**, plus all the other terrific Temptations coming in 1994! Please take the time to write and let me know your thoughts on the books we are selecting for you.

The Editor
Mills & Boon Temptation
Eton House
18-24 Paradise Road
Richmond
Surrey
TW9 1SR

When It's Right

GINA WILKINS

MILLS & BOON LIMITED
ETON HOUSE, 18-24 PARADISE ROAD
RICHMOND, SURREY TW9 1SR

*MILLS & BOON and the Rose Device are trademarks of the
publisher. TEMPTATION is a trademark of Harlequin Enterprises
Limited, used under licence.*

*First published in Great Britain in 1994
by Mills & Boon Limited, Eton House, 18-24 Paradise Road,
Richmond, Surrey TW9 1SR*

© Gina Wilkins 1993

ISBN 0 263 78565 3

21 - 9402

Made and printed in Great Britain

Prologue

DOTTIE LOVELL KNEW how badly her son, Dr. Kane Lovell, wanted a family. She knew he longed for picnics and ball games, first bike rides and school programs. He wanted to tuck his children into bed and then snuggle by a fire with his wife, tell her about his day at the clinic and listen to stories of her day at the office, at home, or whatever she did when they weren't together. And when he was called away on those emergencies that so often interrupted the life of a small-town physician, he wanted to know that he had a real home to return to, not just an empty house and an even emptier bed.

Kane wanted a family. And no one understood that better than his mother, who'd raised him to treasure the most valuable assets of life—love, children, and caring for others.

"We have to help him find a wife who meets all his requirements," she said with a wistful sigh, peering over her teacup at her two silver-haired companions. "The poor darling is so lonely."

Dottie's sister, Mildred Henderson, shook her head in a gesture of exasperation. "He's dated some lovely girls during the past year. And yet he found something wrong with each of them. Maybe he doesn't really want to be married as badly as he says he does."

"Of course he wants to be married!" Dottie argued indignantly. "It's just that he wants the marriage to be a lasting, happy one, as mine was. Cathy hurt him so badly, and he doesn't want that to happen again. He's being careful not to get involved again with someone who's wrong for him."

"Mildred's right, though," Johnnie Mae Harkin chimed in. She was Dottie's best friend. "He's being *too* careful," she continued. "Cathy was a mistake, but you have to admit, Dottie, the women he's dated during the past year were all above reproach. Take Virginia Halstead, for example. She's beautiful, intelligent, successful, and still an old-fashioned young woman who'd love to be married and start a family. Yet Kane dated her only two or three times before all but pushing her into the arms of that handsome attorney she's seeing now."

"And Caroline McElroy," Mildred said, shaking her finger as though in accusation. "A lovely girl. Sings in the church choir and sounds like one of the angels from heaven. Yet Kane introduced her to that new associate minister, and now *they're* engaged. Is Kane really looking for someone for himself, or does he just enjoy matchmaking for others?"

"He just hasn't found the right girl yet," Dottie insisted stubbornly. "There must be one young woman out there who is perfect for my son."

Mildred's rather stern, thin face creased with a frown, then her faded eyes brightened. "Melanie Chastain!"

Her friends looked at her questioningly. "Who?" Dottie asked.

"Melanie Chastain. Pearl's granddaughter. Now that she's moved back from Saint Louis to take over her father's store, she'll be living here full-time and looking to settle down. Melanie would be ideal for Kane. She's bright and pretty and well-bred. She'd make a fine doctor's wife."

"She's a bit young for him, isn't she?" Johnnie Mae asked doubtfully. "Maybe Connie Travers would be better suited. Of course, she does have those three children from her first marriage, but . . ."

"Melanie's twenty-three," Mildred replied. "Only ten years younger than Kane. That's not so much. And she's just the right age to get married and start a family."

Dottie was intrigued. "Maybe we should find a way to introduce them."

Mildred nodded as though the task was already done. "Maybe Melanie will be the one to meet his requirements. I certainly hope so. In a town this small, there aren't that many eligible young women from whom to select."

Johnnie Mae still looked skeptical. "As choosy as that boy is, will we know the right one if we find her?"

"More importantly," Dottie murmured, "will *Kane*?"

1

ALEXANDRA BENNETT had probably had worse days in her life. She simply couldn't remember one, right off-hand.

She was lost on this September Tuesday evening, somewhere in western Mississippi, in a sports car that'd been making an odd noise for the past hour and a half. She'd started out with a map, but had left it in the restaurant where she'd eaten a late lunch, five hours ago. Her head hurt from searching for familiar-sounding road signs, her neck was stiff from hours at the wheel, and to top it all off, light rain had turned into a raging deluge, complete with thunder and lightning and buffeting winds.

She could hardly see the road signs now, much less recognize the names on them. The only building she'd seen in hours was a combination of gas station and truck stop at an intersection some fifteen miles behind her which hadn't looked particularly inviting.

Now she was lost, tired, hungry and irritable. She wondered what on earth had possessed her to leave Chicago and strike out on this impulsive research trip to the so-called Romantic South.

She pressed harder on the accelerator when a faint glimmer of lights flickered through sheets of water. Surely it was a town, she thought, although she hadn't yet spotted any houses. She knew there *were* towns in Mississippi; the whole state wasn't made up of woods, pastures and crop fields. Of course, she wouldn't have bet on that during the past hour or so of driving. If only she could find a map, a decent restaurant and a telephone, she'd be fine.

What she found instead was a cow.

The rather bewildered-looking bovine was standing right in the middle of the road when Alex's sports car rounded the curve. Alex cursed frantically and slammed on the brakes, only to be thrown into a stomach-wrenching spin when the little car skidded on the oily, wet asphalt.

Clinging to the steering wheel with grim determination, she fought to regain control, but the car suddenly left the road and smacked solidly into a muddy ditch, the front right fender slamming into the base of a huge tree.

On impact, Alex's head whipped forward and then to the left, connecting sharply with the side window. The pain left her dazed, her vision blurred, her ears ringing. She felt something warm and wet trickle down her cheek, and for a moment thought the window had broken and the rain was coming in. Then several drops fell onto her hand.

Unless the rain had suddenly turned red—she wouldn't have been surprised if it had, in this gray, deserted world where cows appeared in the middle of roads—she was bleeding.

Great, she thought with a moan, lifting a tentative hand to the throbbing spot on the side of her head. Terrific. Just what she needed.

"Why are you *doing* this to me?" she wailed, looking through the windshield, as if half expecting to find a grinning imp perched in the branches of the tree her car was wrapped around.

Her thoughts slowly cleared. She looked around, taking stock of her situation. Okay, so she wouldn't be driving out of the ditch. The car was pretty well totaled. And she didn't see anyone rushing to help her, so it looked as though it was up to her to take care of herself—as always. The right door was crushed against the tree, the driver's door wedged solidly against an embankment of crumbling mud. Having no intention of being trapped in the car until someone just happened along to rescue her, Alex looked for another way out.

Since there were no other doors available, it appeared that the only thing to do was break out a window. She looked around for a suitable battering tool. Her gaze fell on the metal-cased portable computer in the passenger seat. "No way," she said aloud.

She thought of her shoes, but they were lightweight, Italian leather of little use at the moment. Then she remembered the heavy, six-cell flashlight beneath the seat. She'd always known it would come in handy one day.

Closing her eyes tightly and shielding her face with her left arm, she slammed the end of the flashlight into the back window, without a pang for the damage she was causing. What was a little broken glass, considering the shape the car was in already? She continued to smash the window until pellets of safety glass covered everything in sight, and cold rain poured in through the opening, drenching her. Then she slid her purse strap over her neck, grabbed her computer and clambered awkwardly out of the two-seater, cursing when she snagged her hundred-dollar skirt on something jagged.

Aching, bruised, breathless and still bleeding, she balanced precariously on the tilted surface provided by the trunk, reaching out with one foot to try to find a foothold on the muddy embankment. She'd just managed to step off the car and onto the slippery ground when a cold nose thrust inquisitively against the back of her neck, accompanied by a snuffle of warm, rank-smelling breath.

Alex screamed and flailed her arms, landing on her bottom in three inches of muck. Looking up, she saw two curious, brown eyes watching as she hammered her fists into the mud in a temper tantrum worthy of a spoiled six-year-old.

"You stupid, worthless, undercooked pot roast!" she screamed at the unfazed cow. "This is a three-hundred-dollar jacket! And that's a three-thousand-dollar computer and a thirty-five-thousand-dollar car! I hope someone from Burger King finds you and turns you into Burger Buddies!"

The cow snorted, as if unimpressed by Alex's less than rational tirade.

Alex decided she'd been wrong. She hadn't had a worse day in her life. Sitting in the rain and the mud in rural Mississippi, her clothing ruined, her car smashed, her head bleeding, her computer rusting beneath her hand, and a cow chewing on the hem of her skirt—*this* had to be the lowest point of her life.

"What did I do to deserve this?" she moaned, climbing stiffly, slowly, carefully to her feet.

A zap of lightning overhead, accompanied by a near-deafening clap of thunder, was her only answer. Gripping her purse and computer more firmly, she doggedly struck out in the direction in which she'd been driving, praying that the glimmer of light she'd seen ahead hadn't just been a figment of her imagination. She had to get indoors, and soon, before a bolt of lightning finished the job the car accident had begun.

She could almost see the headlines now. Famous Author Found French-fried. Cow from Hell the Only Witness.

Alex almost thought she was hallucinating when she saw the house. A looming Victorian, set some fifty yards back from the road, surrounded by huge, autumn-nude trees, it looked like the setting for a low-budget, horror movie, particularly when lightning flickered behind it, casting weird shadows in Alex's direction. But there were lights in the windows, so she limped determinedly down the drive, carrying her discarded, useless, mud-caked shoes in her right hand, her computer in her left, her saturated leather purse dangling from her neck.

She didn't care if this place was the Bates Motel, as long as it was dry and warm inside.

It took almost all the energy she had left to struggle up the four steps to the front porch. Her hand was shaking so badly that she missed the doorbell button twice before she managed to press it. A moment later the door opened. A tiny, gray-haired woman in a flowered cotton dress stood in a brightly lighted entryway, staring at Alex in dismay. "Oh, dear," the woman said in a small, high-pitched voice.

Alex knew exactly what she must look like, her dark hair plastered to her head and neck, her face streaked with blood and mud, her clothing wet, torn and filthy, her feet bare except for her torn, sagging stockings. She wouldn't blame the woman for slamming the door in her face. But oh, how she hoped she wouldn't!

"Please," she whispered through cold-stiffened lips. "I had an accident..."

"Oh, you poor dear. Come in, let's get you taken care of. *Kane!*" the woman shouted, her crooning voice suddenly rising to a shriek that made Alex wince. "Kane, we need you! Hurry!"

Alex was dripping miserably upon the polished hardwood floor of the entryway when a man appeared from another room in instant reaction to the woman's cry for help. "Mother? What—?" His gaze landed on Alex. "Oh. Hello."

"It's very nice to meet you," Alex murmured with a sickly attempt at a smile, wondering hazily if he was really drop-dead gorgeous or if her rapidly blurring vision was deceiving her. "I think I'm going to..."

Her voice faded, just as all the lights seemed to blink out at once to pitch her into darkness. Her knees buckled, she thought she heard the gray-haired woman cry out, then there was nothing but silence.

REACTING with well-honed reflexes, Kane reached out as the woman fell, catching her before she hit the floor. She was dripping wet and half-covered with mud, but he gathered her into his arms without hesitation, heedless of his crisp, white shirt and neatly pleated, dark slacks. He noted automatically that she was surprisingly light for a woman so nicely curved. And then he frowned in surprise at the uncharacteristic undoctorlike observation.

A babble of questions came from the three elderly ladies and the beautiful, twenty-three-year-old blonde, who stood in the doorway to the living room. "Who is she?" Kane's Aunt Mildred inquired, staring in astonishment at the unconscious woman in his arms.

"She said she was in an accident," Dottie explained, wringing her hands as she stood by her son. "Oh, dear. What should we do for her, Kane?"

"I need to examine her," he replied, studying the still-oozing wound at the woman's left temple. It topped a nasty, rapidly purpling lump that concerned him much more than the shallow cut. "Where do you want me to put her?"

"The downstairs bedroom," Dottie decided quickly, stepping around him as she spoke. "I'll pull back the bedspread for you. A little dirt won't hurt the sheets."

"What can I do, Kane?" Mildred asked quickly, not wanting to be left out.

"Hot water," Kane answered, already moving to follow his mother, stepping around the shoes and metal case that had hit the floor when the woman fainted. "And Johnnie Mae, you can find something dry for her to wear. We need to get her out of these wet clothes."

His mother's friend nodded and hurried toward the stairs leading up to the second floor, where the occupied bedrooms were located.

"Can I do anything to help, Kane?" Melanie Chastain offered, still standing beside her grandmother, who was watching curiously.

Kane nodded. "If you don't mind getting wet, there's a medical bag in the backseat of my car. The car's not locked."

"I'll get it," she assured him with a smile, already reaching for the doorknob.

"Thanks." Kane thought fleetingly that Melanie seemed like a nice young woman, though he'd known her only a few weeks. Attractive, levelheaded, competent. Didn't seem to mind having their dinner interrupted by this unexpected development, unlike some of the women he'd dated in the past year.

Then the woman in his arms stirred and moaned, and he turned his full attention back to her, laying her gently upon the iron bedstead his mother had readied for her. He snapped on the bedside lamp and turned her face toward it, lifting first one eyelid and then the other to note the reaction of her pupils. He was relieved that both responded exactly as they should.

Her eyes were brown, he noticed. Almost black. So was her hair, though of course it was dripping wet. Would it be lighter when it dried?

He accepted a warm, damp washcloth from his aunt, gently clearing some of the mud from his patient's face. Although she was pale, he thought she might be quite attractive. It was just hard to be sure at the moment.

He looked around when Melanie approached him with the standard black medical bag, hardly a blond hair out of place even after her trip to his car. Obviously, she'd taken time to find an umbrella before going out. "Thanks."

"You're welcome. Is there anything else you need? Would you like us to leave the room now?"

She really had potential, Kane thought approvingly. His eyes still on the injured woman, he nodded. "Why don't you all finish dinner before it gets cold? Mother can help me in here. I'll let you know if I need anything."

Melanie ushered Mildred, Johnnie Mae and her grandmother out of the room with a subtle skill that had Kane smiling as he opened his bag. "Where was she when I was interviewing office nurses?" he asked his mother.

"Earning her business degree at Tulane," Dottie reminded him with a quick smile that faded when she turned back to the bed. "How badly is she hurt, Kane?"

"We're about to find out," he replied, efficiently stripping off the woman's ruined, expensive-looking jacket.

SOMEONE WAS DISTURBING Alex's sleep, making her squirm in discomfort by applying pressure against her bruised ribs and the throbbing lump on her head. She thought she knew who—or what—was being so inconsiderate of her misery. That damned cow.

Something pressed against her left shoulder, and she flinched at the discovery of yet another tender spot. She swatted weakly at the offender. "Get away, you stupid side of beef," she muttered without opening her eyes. "I hope someone barbecues you."

Her growl was answered by a surprisingly masculine chuckle. "Now that's a threat I haven't heard before," a deep voice drawled.

Alex's eyelids flew upward; she blinked frantically against the light that assaulted her. To her relief, a large hand reached out to dim the lamp. She managed to bring the face above her into focus—and what a face it was! "Oh," she said without thinking. "You really *are* gorgeous."

The man's hazel eyes widened fractionally, then crinkled at the corners when he grinned. His mouth was bracketed by deep dimples, his jaw square and faintly cleft. His coffee-colored hair tumbled boyishly onto his forehead, as though he'd been running his hands through it. "Thank you. I'd return the compliment, but I'm afraid you're not looking your best at the moment."

Alex would have bitten her tongue if she hadn't been so reluctant to inflict any more damage on her sore, aching body. She must have hit her head harder than she'd thought!

Then she forgot her embarrassment at her unguarded words. She suddenly realized that she was lying in a strange bed, wearing nothing, it seemed, but her panties and a very thin sheet. And this man was sitting so close that his thigh brushed her hip.

Gorgeous or not, she wasn't at all comfortable with being quite so intimate with a stranger. She drew back. "Er—"

"I'm so glad you're awake, dear. You made us all quite nervous," a woman's voice said from the other side of the bed.

Alex looked around quickly—too quickly; her battered head throbbed in protest. She found the gray-haired lady who'd opened the door standing beside the bed, still wringing her hands and looking worried.

Alex attempted a smile, futilely hoping the fragile-looking woman was the one who'd removed her clothing. "I'm sorry to be so much trouble. I wrecked my car just down the road, and there wasn't anyplace else to go."

"That's quite all right," the woman assured her. "Kane's very good at handling emergencies. He's taking care of you."

Kane? Alex looked back at the man beside her, noting that he was reaching toward the wound on her head. She pulled back again, not trusting him with the painful spot. "Maybe you could call an ambulance or something?" she suggested. "And did you really have to take my clothes off?"

"They were soaked and covered with mud," he answered matter-of-factly. "We'll find you something to wear, once I get you sewn up. I don't really think an ambulance is necessary. It's only a cut, and there's no indication of a concussion. Your shoulder and ribs will be sore for a few days from the bruises you received when your seat belt tightened, but other than that, you'll be fine. You were lucky."

"Yes, I—" Alex stopped talking abruptly when his words finally sank in. "Wait a minute! What do you mean, once you get me sewn up?"

He reached toward a tray that had been set up on the bedside table and lifted a hypodermic needle. "You're going to need a few stitches—three, maybe four. But don't worry about it. The scar will hardly be notice-able. It's a clean split, should be no problem at all."

Alex suddenly remembered her earlier thoughts of the Bates Motel. It hadn't mattered then if there had been a crazy man and his mother inside the warm, dry Victorian house she'd found in the storm. Now she was starting to have second thoughts. "If you think . . ."

"Kane's very good at this," the older woman boasted with a smile. "He hardly ever leaves a scar."

Alex swallowed hard. "Please tell me you're a doc-tor."

He grinned, his sexy mouth tilting to show perfect, white teeth. Alex blinked, thinking again that he was the most beautiful man she'd ever seen—if only he weren't holding that damned syringe.

"Don't worry, I know what I'm doing," he assured her. "I watch a lot of TV. Never miss 'General Hospi-tal.'"

Alex groaned loudly and closed her eyes, making the man laugh. The older woman didn't seem amused. "Honestly, Kane, you're frightening her," she scolded, patting Alex's hand.

"He's only teasing you, dear. My son *is* a doctor, of course—Dr. Kane Lovell. A general practitioner. He and a partner operate a clinic in Andersenville. And I'm his mother, Dottie Lovell. This is my house. The near-est hospital is about twenty miles from here, but we'd be happy to take you there, if you like."

Somewhat reassured, Alex opened her eyes. "It's only a little cut?"

Kane abandoned his teasing and smiled. "Only a lit-tle cut," he repeated. "And a big lump that's more painful than serious. So, what will it be? Want me to take care of it here, or would you like a ride to the hospital?"

Alex frowned, deciding she didn't have a great deal of choice. She just hoped the doctor and his mother hadn't exaggerated his expertise. She wasn't an overly vain woman, but she didn't really want an ugly scar at her temple. "Be careful, okay?"

Kane's smile didn't even waver. "You bet," he assured her, then set to work with sterilizing, alcohol-soaked pads and anesthetics, his touch so gentle and obviously competent that Alex almost sighed in relief.

Wait until she told her friends at home about this adventure! Lost in Mississippi, ambushed by a cow, stripped and sewn by a dream of a country doctor—her friends would never believe it.

Alex could hardly believe it herself.

2

KANE HAD JUST SMOOTHED a neat, white bandage over the still-deadened wound at Alex's temple when someone knocked lightly at the door. Alex made herself glance away from the doctor leaning over her to look curiously toward the door as it opened slowly.

The vision of blond beauty that glided into the room made her squirm uncomfortably beneath her sheet, suddenly vividly, horribly conscious of exactly how battered and bedraggled she must look.

The other woman was clearly several years younger than Alex, who was unenthusiastically facing her thirtieth birthday in a few weeks, several inches taller, and storybook beautiful. Her golden hair was thick, wavy and fell to well below her shoulders. Her face was a perfect oval, her skin porcelain fair. Her eyes were deep blue and sparkled with health, intelligence and good humor. She had a figure some women—Alex included—would have given anything for. And she wore a friendly, dimpled smile that made Alex instinctively like her, even if she secretly would have preferred to detest her.

"Mildred thought our visitor could use a hot cup of tea after being so cold and wet from her accident," the vision said in a voice inevitably husky and melodious. She looked sympathetically at Alex as she carefully balanced a steaming mug between slender hands. "Are you in very much pain?"

Feeling like a heel for her initial reaction, Alex returned the smile and clutched her sheet more tightly under her chin. "No, just a little sore. Dr. Lovell—" *Was this woman his wife?* "—has taken very good care of me."

The woman turned her radiant smile on Kane. "I'm sure he has."

As though a bit embarrassed by the praise, Kane cleared his throat and stood, stepping away from the bed. "I know you'd like to get dressed and drink the tea. Mother, why don't you help—er...I'm afraid we haven't gotten your name," he said, looking at Alex in sudden question.

"I'm Alexandra Bennett," she answered, "and I can't thank you all enough for being so kind to me."

Kane's mother stiffened visibly. "Alexandra Bennett? *The* Alexandra Bennett?"

Alex flushed, particularly when she noticed the quizzical glance Kane sent—first at his mother, and then at herself. Looking the way she must right now, she was hardly in any shape to chat with a fan. She usually preferred to present a more professional appearance when she was being Alexandra, the author, rather than Alex, the person.

Somehow she managed a weak smile. "I'm a writer," she explained to the older woman. "Perhaps that's why you recognize my name?"

Dottie clasped her hands in front of her in apparent delight. "Of *course* I recognize your name! You're my very favorite writer. Wait until Mildred and Johnnie Mae find out who you are—they'll be so thrilled."

Kane looked at Alex again, this time in recognition. "You write the romantic mysteries my mother likes so much."

Though she'd never much liked having her books labeled quite so succinctly, Alex nodded. "I do like to include romance in my books," she admitted.

"And you do it so well," the blonde chimed in politely. "I've enjoyed your work very much, Ms. Bennett."

"Well, of course you have!" Dottie insisted. "After all, she was number two on *The New York Times* bestseller list for weeks and weeks with her last one. *Everyone* read it."

"Not quite everyone," Alex murmured, glancing at Kane to show she had guessed that he hadn't read her books. She smiled at the women. "Thank you for your compliments. And please, call me Alex."

Kane's mother beamed. "You can call me Dottie. And this is Melanie Chastain, a friend of the family's. Oh, I *must* go tell Mildred and Johnnie Mae and Pearl! They'll be so excited." She turned and all but ran from the room.

"Mother!" Kane protested, but too late. He shook his head and looked apologetically at Alex. "I'm sorry. I'm sure you'd appreciate assistance much more than fawning admiration at the moment."

"I'd be happy to give her a hand, Kane," Melanie volunteered.

He smiled and Alex wondered wistfully what it would be like to be the recipient of a smile like that from a man like Kane. Must be nice.

"Thanks, Melanie," he said. "Aunt Mildred left a sweat suit for her across the back of that chair. No sudden movements," he added with a glance at Alex. "And call me if you start feeling dizzy or nauseous."

Alex nodded, one hand still holding the sheet as she self-consciously lifted the other to her matted, dirty hair. "Is it all right to get this bandage wet?" she asked with uncharacteristic meekness. "I'd really like to clean up."

"Wouldn't you rather just lie there and rest awhile?". he asked with a frown. "You don't have to primp for us—we certainly understand."

Rather annoyed by his use of the word "primp," Alex shook her head stubbornly, ignoring the by now familiar throbbing that ensued. "I want to get this mud off. It feels horrible."

He nodded in apparent resignation toward a door at the other side of the room. "There's a bathroom. Try not to get the bandage wet if you can help it. I'll just have to replace it if you do."

"Right," she murmured, anxious for him to leave. She would have preferred total privacy, but suspected Melanie's assistance would be more than welcome, when she managed to struggle to an upright position.

"Now," Melanie said as soon as Kane had left the room. "Drink this, and then we'll see about getting you up."

Alex wasn't normally an obsessively modest woman, but she couldn't help but be self-conscious when she stood unsteadily on her bare feet a few minutes later, wearing nothing but mud and panties. They couldn't have made a more startling contrast if the effort had been deliberate—Alex short, dark and grubby, Melanie tall, fair and impeccable, her dress crisp and beautifully cut.

Alex wasn't accustomed to being at such a disadvantage. She didn't care for the situation in the least.

If Melanie noticed Alex's discomfort, she certainly didn't show it. She competently ushered Alex into the bathroom and left her there with the sweat suit and instructions to call out if she needed any more help. Then she considerately withdrew, promising to stay close at hand in the bedroom.

Reluctantly remembering Kane's orders about keeping the bandage dry, Alex stepped into the glass-walled shower with a mental promise to do her best. But she *was* going to wash her hair, whatever the consequences!

She didn't linger beneath the blessedly hot water, since she found herself annoyingly weak-kneed. She kept one hand on the tiled wall as she turned off the water and dried herself with a soft, fragrantly scented pink towel. The plain blue sweat suit she'd been provided with was too big, but as soft and clean as the towel. She donned it gratefully, pulling the drawstring waistband tight and smoothing the oversize shirt, which fell well below her hips.

She was especially glad to have found a pair of clean, white socks folded with the suit. Even after the hot shower, her feet were freezing! She pulled on the socks and wiggled her toes in relief at the immediate warmth.

Only then did she find the courage to look into the mirror.

It wasn't an encouraging sight. Her wet, dark, chin-length hair, recently permed and cut at one of Chicago's most exclusive salons, hung in tight curls around her face. She tried finger-combing it into her usual style, with little success. Her makeup was gone, leaving her peach-toned skin paler than usual; her brown eyes looked very large and dark in contrast.

"Damn," she grumbled, her morose gaze falling upon the purplish skin around her left eye, just below the bandage-covered lump at her temple. A shiner. Great. Just what she needed to set off her fetching appearance.

She sighed. "All right, Alexandra. Time to go greet your fans," she muttered ironically, making a face at the mirror.

Melanie was perched on the edge of a tiny boudoir chair when Alex walked back into the bedroom. She stood with a relieved smile. "I was just about to check on you. I was beginning to get worried."

Alex smiled in return. "Sorry. I was making an effort to look presentable."

Melanie studied Alex's face. "Your left eye is really swelling. Is it hurting very badly?"

"No, it's fine," Alex lied.

"Would you like to lie down again? Dottie brought fresh sheets, and I changed the bed while you were in the shower."

Alex glanced at the bed, then shook her head. "I'd rather stay up. I'm fine, Melanie. Really."

Seemingly reassured, Melanie gestured toward the bedroom door. "Then would you like to join the others? I believe Kane has gone to check on your car. And he called the police, too, so you'll have an accident report for your insurance company."

"Dr. Lovell's gone out in this weather to check on my car?" Alex repeated in dismay, remembering the driving rain she'd tramped through to the house. "Oh, he shouldn't have bothered."

"It stopped raining fifteen minutes ago," Melanie assured her. "It's still wet and muddy, of course, but it looks like the worst is over."

"I hope you're right," Alex murmured, wondering for the first time what she was going to do now. Would there be a hotel nearby? A taxi to take her there? How long would it take for her to arrange a rental car? Should she offer to pay Kane for his medical attention, or should that, too, be filed with her insurance company?

Never having been in an accident like this before, she had no idea what to do next.

Melanie led her through the tastefully decorated house into a living room, in which four women waited eagerly to make Alex's acquaintance. Bright, curious eyes studied her the moment she stepped into the room. Holding her wet head high, Alex pasted on a smile. "Hello."

Tiny, white-haired Dottie Lovell stepped forward, taking Alex's hand to lead her to a comfortable-looking armchair. "Sit down, dear. Your poor head must be throbbing. Would you like more tea? Can I get you anything else?"

"No, thank you," Alex refused gently, allowing herself to be seated in the chair. She wasn't used to being hovered over quite so solicitously. She'd long been accustomed to taking care of herself—healthy, sick, injured or otherwise.

"Let me introduce you," Dottie said, turning with a rather smug smile to the other women. "This is my sister, Mildred Henderson, and our friends, Johnnie Mae Harkin and Pearl Chastain. Pearl is Melanie's grandmother. Everyone, this is..." She paused for effect, then said, "Alexandra Bennett. The author."

"We're so thrilled to meet you," the heavy set, kind-faced Johnnie Mae enthused. "We've all enjoyed your books very much."

Pearl nodded her silvery head forcefully. A rather vague-looking woman, she didn't look as though she'd have many opinions of her own, much less the courage to express them if she did. "Very much," she parroted Johnnie Mae in a whispery voice.

A sterner, more dour type, tall, thin Mildred seemed less impressed than the others. She looked Alex over slowly, and Alex knew her wet curls, black eye and borrowed, baggy garments were somewhat disillusioning to the woman. "What are you doing in Andersenville?" Mildred asked rather abruptly, peering at Alex through wire-framed glasses. "Aren't you from up north somewhere?"

"Mildred..." Dottie murmured, seemingly resigned to her sister's blunt manner.

Alex didn't take offense. "I'm from Chicago," she explained. "I came South on a research trip for my next book. I planned to spend some time in Jackson or Hattiesburg, but I must have made a wrong turn several hours ago. I was completely lost when I had the accident."

"You're setting your next book in Mississippi?" Johnnie Mae asked with interest.

"Yes. I've never done a Southern setting, and I've always wanted to do so. I thought spending a few weeks in your state would help me write more realistically, as well as giving me more sources for research."

"Mmm." Mildred crossed her arms over her thin chest and frowned. "Never seen a Northerner yet who could write realistically about the South. They never fail to fall into the Faulkner or Williams stereotypes, not to mention mangling the regional dialect."

Alex lifted an eyebrow at the challenge. "I've always made an effort to avoid stereotypes of any kind in my writing," she replied quietly. "I have no intention of imitating either Faulkner or Williams in my book."

"Don't get Aunt Mildred started on negative Southern stereotypes," a man's voice said from the doorway to Alex's left. "You set her off, you're liable to be listening to her till midnight. She's a bit rabid about the subject."

Alex glanced around at Kane, who entered the room with a uniformed policeman on his heels. Kane looked damp and disheveled, his once-neat clothing liberally splattered with mud. Alex knew the splotches on his formerly white shirt had come from her, when he'd carried her to the bedroom. She squirmed in embarrassment.

She was surprised to see that Kane was carrying a familiar-looking suitcase in each hand. "You brought my luggage," she said unnecessarily.

He nodded. "You left your keys in the ignition, so I was able to open the trunk. Your car will have to be towed out of the ditch. Joe, here, has already radioed for a wrecker."

Joe? Alex looked at the police officer. His broad, dark face lit up with a friendly smile. "Ma'am," he said, giving her a nod of greeting. "I'm Officer Joe Wilson. That nice little car of yours is a goner, I'm afraid. You were dam—" He swallowed, shooting a quick, apologetic look at the ladies watching him. "—er—darned lucky not to have been seriously injured."

Alex nodded. "Yes, I know. I hope someone got that cow locked up before it causes another accident."

Kane and the officer exchanged puzzled glances. "Cow?" Wilson repeated, looking back at Alex. "What cow?"

"The one that ran me off the road," she answered, surprised that they hadn't seen it. "I came around the curve and there it was. If I hadn't taken the ditch, I'd have hit it."

"We didn't see a cow," Kane explained. "No sign of one, either, though I suppose the rain could have washed away tracks."

"Trust me. I may be a city girl, but I know a cow when I see one," Alex said dryly.

Officer Wilson made a note on the report in his hand. "Cow," he murmured. "Can you describe it?"

Alex shrugged. "Black and white. Four legs, two eyes, two ears and a tail. And very bad breath," she added, remembering when the beast had stuck its nose into her face and made her fall.

Kane made a sound that could have been a swallowed laugh, though he tried to look innocent when she shot him a scowl.

Alex spent the next ten minutes answering questions for the accident report, digging into the purse Dottie found for her to produce her driver's license and insurance information. Her head was pounding in earnest by the time the officer seemed satisfied with the information she'd given him.

As though sensing her pain, Kane disappeared for a few moments, to return with two capsules and a glass of water. "Mild pain pills," he explained, putting them into her hand. "They'll probably make you drowsy. When's the last time you had anything to eat?"

"I had a late lunch—maybe one o'clock," she replied, closing her fingers around the capsules. "And I'd rather not take these now. I don't want to be woozy when I need to be making arrangements for where I'm going to stay tonight."

"You're going to stay here, of course," Dottie said immediately, her tone brooking no argument. "Mildred and Johnnie Mae and I all live here. The bedroom you were in earlier is a spare. We'd be honored to have you as our guest tonight, wouldn't we, girls?"

Johnnie Mae bobbed her head in avid agreement. Even Mildred nodded, though not as fervently. "You'd be welcome," she said with apparent sincerity.

Alex didn't cry easily, but she felt tears prick behind her eyelids at their generosity. "Thank you," she murmured. "You've all been very kind to me."

"Southern hospitality," Kane said with a smile. "That's no stereotype."

"Not for most folks, anyway," Mildred added. "Though we have our share of sleazebags."

"Sleazebags?" Dottie repeated with distaste. "You've been watching too much television again, Mildred."

Alex swallowed a chuckle, thinking that she could use characters like these in her book. Maybe Andersenville—wherever the heck it was—wouldn't be a bad place to start her research.

Promising that someone would be in touch with her the next day, Officer Wilson left. Kane was still frowning at Alex. "Take the pills," he ordered her. "Then I want you to eat something, and get a good night's rest. Mother?"

"I'll fix her a plate," Dottie said, appearing to know what he wanted. She headed for the kitchen.

"Bossy type, aren't you?" Alex observed, giving Kane a dry look.

He grinned unrepentently. "You could say that."

"I just did," she reminded him, making him chuckle.

Melanie rose abruptly from the couch, where she'd been sitting with her grandmother. "It's getting late. We should be going."

Alex sat quietly in her chair as Melanie and Pearl took their leave of the others. She watched with particular interest when Melanie stepped to Kane's side to exchange a few words of parting with him.

The tall, dark man and the slender blonde made a handsome couple, she thought grudgingly. So poised and attractive and self-possessed, they looked almost like royalty—a fairly apt analogy for a small-town doctor and his companion, she supposed.

Yet, as lovely a picture as they made standing side by side, something seemed to be missing. Some spark or bond—a sense of intimacy. Or was that bump on the head the only reason for her wild assumptions?

Speaking of a relationship with something missing, she really should call Bill, the man she'd been unenthusiastically dating for the past six months, just to let him know what had happened and where she was staying tonight. She'd like to think that someone out there cared where she was and whether she was all right.

Now didn't *that* sound self-pitying? She almost shook her head in disgust. Just because she'd had a rough day, it didn't mean she was about to spend the rest of the evening moping and feeling sorry for herself!

"I've warmed some of our leftovers from dinner for you." Dottie broke into Alex's thoughts with a kind smile. "Would you like to eat at the table, or would you prefer for me to bring you a tray?"

"The table," Alex returned promptly.

Kane tapped her on the shoulder. "You still haven't taken the pain pills."

She sighed and made a production of swallowing the pills with the water he'd brought her. "There. Are you satisfied?"

He grinned, not bothering to answer. Instead, he glanced at his mother. "I'm going home now. Thanks to the Lawson baby's early arrival, it's been a long day for me. Give me a call if you need anything, okay?"

"We'll be fine, darling. You get some rest," Dottie answered warmly, going up on tiptoe to kiss his cheek.

Kane hugged his aunt, then Johnnie Mae, before turning back to Alex. "I live next door," he told her. "I can be here in just a few minutes if you need me."

"Thank you, but I'll be fine."

He nodded. "You'd better go ahead and eat. Then try to get some sleep."

She thought again that he seemed to be accustomed to giving orders, and to having them obeyed without question. Alex wasn't in the habit of taking orders, not from anyone. But her head was still hurting, she was hungry, and the thought of a good night's sleep was strongly appealing so she decided not to argue with him. This time, at least.

THE HOUSE SEEMED oddly quiet when Kane left, even though Alex's three hostesses all talked quite a bit; they hovered over her while she ate the excellent meal Dottie had warmed up. They'd all read her books, so her work provided the main topic of conversation, which Alex didn't mind; she always enjoyed talking about her books to serious readers.

Johnnie Mae changed the subject when she suddenly frowned and murmured, "Oh, dear!"

"What is it, Johnnie?" Dottie inquired.

Johnnie Mae glanced toward the ceiling, as though looking into her bedroom. "I forgot to ask Kane about Cujo. I'm sure he'd know what I could feed him until the pet store gets some more baby mice."

Alex nearly choked on a mouthful of glazed carrots.

Mildred glowered. "Why on earth you agreed to keep that thing for the next three weeks is beyond me. Don't know how you can sleep, with it crawling around in your room."

"Now, Mildred, you know how fond of his pet Jason is. I couldn't say no when he asked me to take care of it, while he's off on that college study trip. Besides, it's not as if the thing is actually loose in my room."

Dottie made a face. "Just don't ask any of us to go in there until it's gone," she said flatly. "And if it gets loose, there's gonna be heck to pay around here, and that's for sure."

Alex couldn't hold back another minute. "Just—mmm—what are we talking about here?" she asked warily, glancing at the ceiling in imitation of Johnnie Mae.

Johnnie Mae chuckled and patted Alex's hand. "It's only Cujo. My nephew's pet tarantula. A Mexican red, I believe he called it."

"Tar—" Alex shuddered. "Tarantula?"

"Oh, don't worry, dear. Jason assured me it's quite tame. And it's safely closed into a large, glass aquarium in my room. It couldn't *possibly* get loose," Johnnie Mae added with a firm look at Dottie.

She sighed. "I just wish the pet store hadn't run out of baby mice. The owner assured me Cujo doesn't need to eat until he gets more, but I don't know. . . . He looks hungry to me. I'm sure Kane would know what to do. Maybe I'll call him."

"You leave Kane alone," Mildred retorted. "He's worn out, poor thing. Probably already asleep. Besides, he's a doctor, not a veterinarian. What would he know about feeding spiders?"

Alex shivered again and surreptitiously pushed away her plate, unable to touch the few bites of food left on it. She'd suddenly lost her appetite.

"I suppose you're right," Johnnie Mae conceded reluctantly. She thought a moment, then cocked her head. "Wonder if he'd like a few bugs?"

This time it was Dottie who firmly changed the subject. "We should let Alex finish her coffee," she chided Mildred and Johnnie Mae. "She's had a rough day and needs to get to bed."

Johnnie Mae and Mildred nodded, joining Dottie in the kitchen that adjoined the dining room. Sipping the last of the excellent decaffeinated coffee Dottie had poured for her, Alex could hear them talking through the open doorway while they cleaned up.

"Dinner went well, didn't it?" Johnnie Mae asked.

"Very nice," Dottie agreed. "Pearl was so proud to be able to show off her granddaughter."

"A lovely girl," Mildred pronounced in her firm tone. "Such nice manners, too. You don't find many like her these days."

Hoping she was unobserved, Alex made a face and swallowed the last of her coffee. Melanie had seemed nice enough, but surely she wasn't *that* perfect!

"I think he was interested," Johnnie Mae said, making Alex listen more intently.

"He did look interested," Mildred agreed. "Especially when she was so quick to help with Alex. She'd make a good wife for a doctor."

"Kane did seem to like Melanie," Dottie murmured, her words just audible to Alex. "But I'm not sure there was anything more to it than that. He wasn't . . . Well, I suppose we'll just have to wait and see."

Alex frowned. So that was the situation, she thought. The ladies were matchmaking.

It wasn't any of her business, of course, but Alex tended to agree with Dottie. There *hadn't* been any real sparks between the handsome doctor and the beautiful blonde. Side by side, they'd radiated about as much seething, sexual intensity as . . . well, as Barbie and Ken.

But still, who was she to judge? If she'd decided for some reason that Kane and Melanie weren't quite right for each other, it was only because she didn't know any of them well enough to draw conclusions. What else could it be?

"Is there anyone you'd like to call, Alex?" Dottie asked some twenty minutes later, after escorting Alex back to the bedroom she'd be using for the night. Dottie gestured toward the telephone on the nightstand. "Please feel free to use the phone to call your family. Won't they be worried about you?"

Alex shook her head cautiously, one hand pressed lightly to the bandage at her temple. The pain had dulled, but the medication was already making her drowsy. She couldn't wait to crawl back into that wonderfully comfortable, old-fashioned bed.

"Both my parents died several years ago, and I don't really have any other family to worry about me," she assured the older woman. "I have a couple of friends in Chicago who know I'm away, but I don't check in every day. I'll call someone tomorrow and let them know what happened."

"No family," Dottie repeated softly, her eyes sympathetic. "How sad for you."

Alex managed a smile. "I've been on my own a long time, ever since I graduated from high school. I'm perfectly capable of looking out for myself, Dottie."

"I'm sure you are," Dottie answered. "But . . ."

She stopped and shook her head. "Sorry. I'm afraid I'm rather old-fashioned when it comes to family. My own daughter—Kane's older sister—calls home once a week, even though she's been married and living in West Virginia for the past ten years."

"That's nice," Alex assured her with a sleepy smile. "You're obviously very close to both your children." She was aware of a touch of envy as she spoke. She'd never been very close to her own parents, though they'd all tried hard enough over the years.

"Very close. Now, can I get you anything else before you turn in?"

"No, really, you've done more than enough. I don't know how to thank you for—"

"Don't be silly," Dottie broke in firmly. "I've considered it an honor. Don't be afraid to call out if you need anything during the night, you hear? The girls and I sleep upstairs, but we'll be down in a snap if you need us."

Alex nodded, rather relieved when Dottie left the room. She really wasn't accustomed to so much attention. When she'd been sick as a child, her nannies had offered the "chin-up-and-stiff-upper-lip" sort of comfort. Her brilliant, workaholic parents had tried to offer commiseration, but hadn't been very skilled at communicating with a sick child, no matter how much they might have wanted to do so. She'd understood— but at times she'd longed for more.

She'd bet Dottie's children had been given special treatment when they'd been sick—hot soup, hugs, the feel of a soft, loving hand stroking their fevered cheeks. Things Alex had so often fantasized about when she was younger, before she'd outgrown such futile dreams.

She changed into the nightgown she'd taken from her suitcase and climbed into bed, settling her tender head upon the pillow with a long sigh. What a day. She needed a good night's rest to face the morning, and all the decisions and arrangements waiting to be made then. Tonight she was even too tired to worry about whether Cujo would get hungry enough to attempt a breakout!

She drifted almost immediately into sleep, wondering if she'd be seeing Kane the next day. And she wondered why the thought of him brought a faint smile to her lips.

KANE FOUND HIMSELF AWAKE at just before one in the morning. Making a face at the dry taste in his mouth, he crawled out of bed and headed for the kitchen, where he ran tap water into a glass and downed it without coming up for air. He wiped his mouth with the back of his hand and set the glass upon the counter, glancing idly out the window over the sink toward his mother's house next door. Security lamps in both yards made it easy for him to see that everything looked normal, quiet—all the lights were out in his mother's house, as he'd expected at this hour.

He realized that his attention had focused on the spare bedroom's window. How comfortable was Alexandra Bennett in her strange surroundings? Was she in pain from her injuries?

She'd been fortunate not to have been more seriously hurt in the accident. He remembered with an uncomfortable pang the condition of the expensive little car he'd found crumpled in that ditch. She'd shown spunk to break out of the wrecked vehicle and make her way to the nearest house through the storm with her head dripping blood.

He told himself to go back to bed. Alex was fine, of course. No serious injuries, no sign of concussion. Nothing at all for him to worry about.

But he couldn't help thinking how small and pale and bedraggled she'd looked when she'd collapsed into his arms.

Wet, muddy, injured and all, something about Alex had appealed to his most basic, male instincts from the moment he'd seen her... And then, she'd opened her eyes and artlessly told him he was gorgeous. There was just something about her...

"Well, hell," he muttered. He sighed deeply and headed for his own bedroom, calling himself several unflattering names along the way.

3

"ALEX? ALEX, can you open your eyes?" The voice was quiet, deep, slipping gently into her dreams to rouse her without startling her.

Alex stirred against the pillow; who was trying to wake her?

"Alex? Come on, honey, open your eyes."

Honey? No one called her "honey!" She frowned and reluctantly forced her heavy eyelids upward, surprised to find Kane Lovell sitting on the edge of the bed beside her. The room was dark except for the dimly burning lamp on the bedside table.

"What are you doing?" she mumbled, hearing her voice hoarse from sleep. "What time is it?"

"Just after one in the morning," he answered rather apologetically. "Look straight ahead for me, okay?"

Realizing she'd been asleep less than four hours—no wonder she still felt so tired!—she didn't move when he shone a tiny light into her right eye, then into her left, watching her intently as he did so.

"Good," he said, snapping off the penlight. "Is your head hurting? I can give you something else for pain now if you need it."

Her mind still clouded with sleep, she tried to think. "No. It feels better. I didn't expect you tonight."

"I know. I just wanted to check on you."

She blinked and rubbed one hand across her eyes, wincing when she brushed the sore flesh of her bruised left cheek. She noted that Kane was wearing a gray sweat suit and that his dark hair was rumpled, as though he'd just climbed out of bed, himself. Why had he interrupted his sleep to come back out and check on her? "Do you do this sort of thing often?"

"Take care of my patients?" He smiled a little as he stashed the penlight in his bag. "It's what I do for a living, remember?"

"I meant, make house calls," she clarified, running a hand through her tousled hair. "Is that a regular practice for you?"

"It's my mother's house. And I live less than a hundred yards away. No big deal."

"Does your mother know you're here?"

"No. Everyone's asleep. I let myself in with my key."

"Why?" Alex asked, genuinely curious and a bit concerned that he'd gone to that much trouble. "Do I have a concussion or something?"

He smiled reassuringly and shook his head. "I didn't see any signs of concussion earlier. But I got up for a drink of water a few minutes ago and thought I might as well check on you while I was up. Sorry I bothered you. You can go back to sleep now. You're going to be fine."

Alex wondered bemusedly if this sort of behavior was common in small-town Mississippi. A doctor who interrupted a much-needed night's sleep, just to check on a patient who was a virtual stranger to him? She would never have believed it!

"'Curiouser and curiouser,'" she murmured with a shake of her head, quoting from *Alice's Adventures in Wonderland*.

Kane chuckled. "What are you describing?"

"My life," she explained, returning his smile. "Ever since I misplaced my map and got lost and then ambushed by a cow, strange things have been happening to me."

His grin deepened. He'd started to rise a moment earlier, but now he settled back on the bed, one hand draped loosely over his knee as he looked at her. "Are you referring to me as one of those strange things?"

"Maybe." Their eyes locked and her smile faded. It suddenly occurred to her that it was the middle of the night, she was lying in bed, wearing her favorite, thin silk nightgown, the room was quiet and shadowed, and an utterly gorgeous man was looking down at her with a smile that made her toes curl beneath the sheet.

Talk about a great bedside manner!

She blinked and cleared her throat, strictly damping down an attack of demented hormones. Bad timing. Wrong man. But, oh, what an interesting specimen he was!

She tried for a moment to picture Bill, the man she'd been dating in Chicago, who'd recently asked her to marry him. And though she'd actually been considering accepting that proposal, she found it impossible to bring a clear image of him to her mind now.

She'd known there'd been a depressing lack of passion in their relationship, but hadn't quite realized what had been missing. She'd never looked up at Bill and quite literally felt her heart in her throat as she did now, with Kane Lovell smiling at her, so close she could reach out and touch him.

What was going on here? She didn't even know him! Instant desire wasn't her style, casual intimacy not to her taste. It could only be a case of attraction—mixed, perhaps, with gratitude. It couldn't possibly be anything more than that.

Could it?

No, of course not, she assured herself firmly. She pulled the sheet to her chin. "Thank you for being concerned about me, Dr. Lovell," she said, just a bit too formally. "But I'm fine. Really."

"It's Kane. And I know you're fine," he returned easily, rising in response to her less than subtle hint. "Good night, Alex. I've left two more pain capsules on the nightstand if you should want them later. Don't hesitate to take them if you need them. They won't hurt you, and it's only natural that you should feel some pain from your injury."

"Thank you," she said again, anxious now for him to leave, knowing she wouldn't take a full breath until he did. She'd suddenly discovered the meaning of hyperventilation. She wondered wryly what his medical opinion would be, should she mention that disturbing development. "Good night, Kane."

He smiled and touched her cheek before turning out the light. The touch wasn't as impersonal and professional as she'd expected, but neither could it be construed as presumptuous. Alex was still trying to decide exactly what it *had* been when he let himself out of the bedroom, leaving her staring into the darkness after him.

Just a friendly gesture, that was all, she decided after a moment. What else could it have been?

But her own fingers were still pressed against the spot he'd touched when she finally drifted back to sleep.

DOTTIE HUNG UP the kitchen extension and turned toward the small table, where her housemates were finishing their breakfasts. "That was Kane," she told them, sliding into her own chair. "Very interesting."

Johnnie Mae looked up from her calorie-dripping, cheese Danish. "What was very interesting?"

"Kane just told me he let himself in our house at one o'clock this morning," Dottie announced, watching the other two women expectantly. "He called to make sure he hadn't disturbed anyone."

"Why was Kane here at that hour?" Mildred asked, frowning in curiosity.

Dottie waited just a moment, making sure she had their full attention, then replied, "He said he was worried about Alex. He wanted to check on her."

Johnnie Mae smiled and cut into her pastry again. "He's such a sweet boy."

"Too dedicated for his own good," Mildred muttered, dipping into her bowl of granola and sliced strawberries. "Needs to get more rest. We could've checked on the girl for him."

Exasperated that Mildred and Johnnie Mae hadn't reacted the way she'd wanted, Dottie set down her fork, letting her scrambled eggs congeal on her plate. "Of course, Kane's a very dedicated doctor, but don't you think it's odd that he came over in the middle of the night, just to check on Alex? After all, she only had a small cut on her head. He said there was no sign of a concussion. So why do you suppose he was so concerned about her, hmm?"

Johnnie Mae swallowed the last bite of her pastry and eyed Dottie. "You think there was more to it than professional interest?"

"Could be," Dottie mused. "There *was* something in his voice when he talked about her, something that made me wonder if he's more interested than he'd admit. Maybe more interested than he realizes himself."

"Oh, I don't know, Dottie," Johnnie Mae replied slowly, pushing her empty plate away. "She hardly seems his type."

"And what about Melanie?" Mildred demanded, setting her spoon down with a thump. "I still say she's the one for him. Didn't you see how well she responded to the medical emergency last evening? She's a natural doctor's wife if I ever saw one. And think about it. She was brought up as a Southern lady. She cooks, she makes her own clothes, she teaches Sunday School and takes such good care of her grandmother. As young as she is, she runs her daddy's store like she was born to take over a retail business. I'd say she's just about perfect."

"And as much as I love Melanie, her near perfection is the one thing that makes her wrong for Kane," Dottie replied. "He needs someone to keep him on his toes, someone to take his mind off his work at times. Someone to keep him cut down to size when he starts getting a bit arrogant—as we all know my boy tends to do, at times. Someone like . . . Alex."

"Poppycock. Melanie is much more suitable for him. They make a delightful couple."

"But you saw the way Kane was with her, Mildred," Dottie argued. "No sparks. No sizzle. That's not what we want for him . . . or what he wants for himself."

"Still," Johnnie Mae seemed compelled to point out, "the sparks could develop later. Last night was hardly a private, intimate evening for a romance to develop."

"That's true, of course," Dottie conceded. "But the way he talked this morning . . . I think it's more than professional interest with Alex."

"I think you're wrong," Mildred insisted. "Melanie is . . ."

"Mmm . . . shouldn't this decision be left to Kane?" Johnnie Mae asked tentatively.

Dottie and Mildred looked at her with what might have been interpreted as pity by someone less generous than Johnnie Mae. "He's a man," Mildred said in her usual, blunt manner. "We all know that men don't always know what's best for them."

"It never hurts to give them a little push," Dottie murmured, in rare agreement with her sister. "Maybe we should try a little experiment. You know, just to see if I'm right, and if there's a possibility Alex and Kane could be right for each other."

"What kind of experiment?" Mildred demanded skeptically.

Dottie waved her hand in a vague gesture. "I don't know. A test of some sort, I suppose. Something that would tell us whether Alex could handle being the wife of a small-town doctor."

"Doesn't seem likely," Johnnie Mae said with a sigh and a shake of her head. "After all, she's a famous writer, used to living in a big city. Probably has a very active social life, lots of parties and that sort of thing. What could Andersenville have to offer her?"

"We have a social life," Dottie replied defensively. "Why, there's the church social tonight, for example. Alex might just fit right in."

"Or she may stick out like a sore thumb," Mildred retorted. "The same way Cathy did when Kane would bring her to visit."

"Only one way to find out, isn't there?" Dottie asked, her mind already whirling with possibilities.

"I'd hate to see Kane get hurt again by falling for someone who's wrong for him," Johnnie Mae said. "We really should try to lead him to Connie Travers if nothing happens with Melanie. Her children are very well behaved, and Kane has always liked children."

Mildred stubbornly crossed her arms over her skinny chest. "And I still say Melanie's the one. Just wait till tonight. You'll see how well *she* fits in with our friends and neighbors. After all, she was raised here."

Dottie began to smile. "This should prove to be very interesting."

She saw Johnnie Mae and Mildred exchange glances, then look back at her with bemused expressions.

IT WAS AFTER NINE when Alex woke. The house was quiet, so quiet she wondered if she was alone.

She climbed out of bed, ignoring the pain pills still lying on her nightstand, showered quickly and pulled on a mauve silk sweater and gray slacks. Quick use of her curling iron tamed some of the frizz, and she did her best with makeup, though there was little she could do about the vivid, multicolored bruise covering a good portion of the left side of her face.

"Better," she decided, critically eyeing the reflection in the mirror. "Not great, by any means, but definitely better than last night."

Feeling ready to face the world again, she left her borrowed bedroom in search of her hostesses.

The living room was empty. A faint sound from the kitchen beckoned her in that direction. She found Dottie there, humming an old gospel song as she industriously cleaned countertops. "Good morning."

Dottie turned with a bright smile. "Good morning, Alex. You look much better! How do you feel?"

"Better, thank you."

"Hungry?"

"A bit," Alex admitted.

"Pour yourself a cup of coffee and sit down. I'll fix you something. How about a whole-grain waffle with fresh fruit?"

"I really hate for you to go to so much trouble," Alex fretted.

Dottie only smiled more broadly and shook her head. "I don't mind. Really." And it was obvious that she didn't.

"Where are the others?" Alex asked casually as she followed Dottie's instructions and took a place at the kitchen table with her coffee.

"They both left a while ago. Mildred volunteers two days a week at the regional hospital—the one I mentioned being twenty miles from here. And Johnnie Mae works as a customer greeter at Wal-Mart. She loves doing that."

An active group, apparently, Alex mused, even more interested in the women who had so intrigued her the night before. "You said this is your house?"

Dottie nodded. "My husband and I raised our children here. He passed away ten years ago and my sister, Mildred, moved in with me. Then five years ago, Johnnie Mae, who's been my best friend since childhood, lost her husband, and we persuaded her to join us here. It works out very well for us."

"It's nice for you that your son lives close by," Alex murmured, looking at her coffee cup as she spoke.

"Yes. Kane built his house next door when he set up his practice here a few years back, after finishing his medical training. He likes to think he's keeping an eye on the three of us, but we make sure he eats right and gets as much rest as possible, so there's some question as to who's actually watching out for whom," Dottie explained with a twinkle in her eyes.

Alex smiled, hoping her unexpected wistfulness didn't show in her expression. How she would have liked to belong to a close family, a family that took care of each other, that would always be there in time of need. She had never been first in anyone's life, and it was the one thing she'd always longed for. One reason she'd dated Bill for so long was that he had been flatteringly attentive from their first date, almost smotheringly so.

"I talked to Kane this morning," Dottie said, seemingly out of the blue, making Alex start at the mention of his name.

It wasn't as though she'd been thinking of him, she assured herself quickly, so why did she have the odd feeling that Dottie had read her mind? "Did you?"

"Yes. He asked about you. He said to let you sleep as long as you could. He told me about disturbing you in the night. I hope he didn't frighten you."

"No, not at all. He was very careful not to do so. It was nice of him to be concerned enough about me to come out in the middle of the night like that."

Dottie placed a well-filled plate upon the table, and for a fleeting moment Alex thought the older woman's expression was rather speculative. Then her friendly smile returned and Dottie slid into a chair across the table after pouring herself a cup of coffee.

"My son *is* a very dedicated doctor," she murmured, watching Alex closely over her cup. "Still . . ." But she broke off whatever she'd been going to say by taking a sip of her coffee, to Alex's mild disappointment.

When Dottie spoke again, it was to change the subject completely. "What are you planning to do today, Alex?"

Alex made a face and reached for her coffee. "I suppose I'd better get in touch with my insurance agent first thing. I'll need to arrange for a rental car and a place to stay. And I'd probably better call my—er, a friend in Chicago to let him know what happened and that I'm all right."

"A boyfriend?" Dottie inquired, suddenly frowning.

Alex shrugged. "I've dated him for a while. I don't know that you'd call him a boyfriend, exactly."

"So it's not serious?" Again, Dottie seemed very curious.

Alex had discovered that Southerners seemed quite interested in the lives of everyone they met, so had not been startled when several waitresses and a clerk in a service station had blithely chatted about personal business while they'd waited on her. Now she assumed Dottie's questioning was simply more of the same. And, since she found herself liking Dottie Lovell very much, Alex answered more candidly than she normally would have to a near stranger. "It's serious for him. For me...well, I don't know. I can't seem to make up my mind. That's one of the reasons I decided to make this research trip. I needed some time away."

"Very wise," Dottie said approvingly. "It sounds to me as though he isn't right for you."

Alex blinked at the older woman's vehemence, then laughed weakly. "How could you possibly know that? I haven't told you anything about him."

Dottie didn't seem fazed. "I could tell by the way you spoke about him. He doesn't stir your blood, does he?"

Unable to resist a giggle at the matter-of-fact tone in which Dottie asked the fanciful question, Alex shook her head. "I'm not sure how to answer that. I'm...fond of Bill. I just don't think I'm passionately in love with him," she added, sobering.

"Then he *is* wrong for you," Dottie answered rather sternly. "Don't tie yourself to a union with no passion, Alex. You deserve more than that."

Again, Alex couldn't be offended by the personal remarks. "You sound as though you speak from experience."

Dottie nodded slowly. "I was married very young, to a man my father chose for me. It was . . . a joyless experience," she said after a momentary pause. "He was killed in an industrial accident three years into our marriage, leaving me determined never to marry again. And then I met Charles—Kane and Debbie's father. He convinced me to try again, showed me how glorious love could be. The twenty-six years I had with him were the happiest years of my life."

"You miss him, don't you?" Alex asked softly, reading the sadness in Dottie's eyes.

The older woman sighed and nodded. "Very much. He died quite unexpectedly. I'd hoped to have more time with him. But I can't regret anything. We had a strong, loving, passionate marriage. That's what I always wanted for my children. Debbie seems to have found it with her husband, though Kane hasn't yet been as fortunate. And I'd like the same for you, Alex."

"Why me?" Alex couldn't help asking, surprised by the sincerity in Dottie's voice.

Dottie smiled. "I like you," she answered simply.

Strange how the simple statement shook Alex so deeply. "I like you, too," she said, her throat tight.

"I'm glad. And you'll think about what I said? I mean, if you were to meet someone who *did* stir your blood, someone who could offer more than a comfortable, practical arrangement, you'd be interested, wouldn't you?"

Alex squirmed restlessly in her seat, wondering if Dottie had anyone in particular in mind. But that was absurd, of course. Dottie was simply being nice. Wasn't she?

"Of course, I'll think about what you said," she promised, without really answering the question, avoiding Dottie's eyes by concentrating on her breakfast.

"Good. Now, about your plans," Dottie said briskly. "I wonder if I could convince you to stay here for a while. If you want to research a genuine Southern town, Andersenville is a perfect example. And you should take it easy for a few more days to give yourself a chance to fully recover from your accident. And finally, Mildred and Johnnie Mae and I would be delighted to have you here. Please consider it."

Alex was strongly tempted. "If I stay," she said slowly, "I would insist on paying room and board. I refuse to take any further advantage of your generosity."

"It isn't necessary, but if it would make you more comfortable, we'll work something out," Dottie agreed.

"I *could* set up my computer at the desk in the bedroom you've provided me," Alex murmured, thinking how inviting the small, but functional antique desk had looked that morning.

"Then there's no problem at all, is there?" Dottie asked brightly, seeming to assume the matter was settled.

Alex bit her lip, wondering why she'd suddenly thought of Kane at the mention of the word "problem." Why should Dottie's son be a problem? Just because she'd found herself attracted to him in the middle of the night was no reason to turn down the opportunity to stay in an ideal place, while researching her new book and working up a proposal for her publisher.

She probably wouldn't even feel the same way if she should see him again now, in broad daylight; the trauma of her accident was dissipating quickly. And he probably hadn't given her more than a passing thought since he'd left her early this morning. So why should she be concerned about her reaction to him—or vice versa?

No, Kane Lovell had absolutely nothing to do with this, she decided, nodding in sudden decision. "All right, Dottie. I appreciate your offer. I'd like to spend some time here, as long as you allow me to pay a fair amount of room and board while I'm here."

Dottie's smile was almost blindingly brilliant. "I'm so glad," she murmured, clapping her hands. "This should be extremely interesting."

IF KANE HADN'T GIVEN his word to his mother that he would attend the church social Wednesday evening, he would have found any excuse not to go.

He was tired, hungry, and a bit cross and really wanted to head home, kick off his shoes and crash in front of a PBS special on TV. His mother regularly made up her own frozen TV dinners for him and stacked them in his freezer, so all he had to do was stick one into the microwave to have a delicious, home-cooked meal, complete with meat and steaming vegetables. He even had a fairly decent wine he'd bought on impulse a few days ago.

He sighed wistfully at the vision of himself in a sweat suit, with one of those dinners, a glass or two of that wine and his television set. A perfect evening. And yet here he was, still wearing his tie and pulling into one of the few remaining parking spaces in front of the First Baptist Church. All because of a promise his mother had wheedled out of him in a weak moment. *Sucker.*

"Hey, Kane! How's it goin'?" a man called to him, almost the minute he climbed out of his car.

Kane waved a greeting at the heavyset farmer, standing with a couple of other men who were having a smoke in the parking lot. "Goin' just fine, Zeb. When you going to listen to me and cut out those cigarettes?"

"Real soon, Doc," Zeb promised with a patently insincere smile. "And I'm gonna' start that diet Monday."

"Yeah, right," Kane muttered, knowing the man would do nothing of the sort, despite having high blood pressure and a cholesterol count that made Kane shudder. Zeb and his family would expect Kane to work a miracle when Zeb's overworked heart finally rebelled. And Kane would try his best to cooperate.

"Dr. Lovell! I'm so glad you're here." A tall, big-bosomed woman in a brightly flowered dress and a precariously perched hat tugged imperiously at Kane's arm.

"I'm still having trouble sleeping," she told him, lowering her booming voice to a stage whisper. "Haven't had a good night's rest since 1978. Couldn't you please prescribe something else for me? Just a few pills to help me out a bit?"

"I've told you, Madelyn, regular exercise would help you much more than another prescription for sleeping pills," Kane answered, as gently as he could. "I really don't think it's in your best interest to prescribe more medication at this time."

Her face fell, though she knew better than to argue with him. "Whatever you think best, Doctor."

He patted her hand. "Come see me in a few days if you're still having trouble," he advised. "We'll see what we can do."

She sighed and drifted away. Kane knew he'd be seeing her within a week; she'd be asking again for a prescription that he couldn't in all conscience provide her with. That, too, was a part of his job.

"Hi, Doc! Where's your needles?" a broad-faced, gap-toothed boy asked cheerfully, pausing for a moment in a game of tag with several other children in the church playground.

"Left them in my car, Paul," Kane returned without missing a beat, "but I'll pull them out, just for you, if you're feeling poorly."

Wide-eyed, Paul protectively covered his blue-jeaned bottom with both hands and shook his sandy head. "No, thanks, Dr. Lovell. I'm feeling just fine."

Kane laughed. "Glad to hear it."

He took a deep breath and entered the social hall of the church, knowing he was in for more of the same for the next couple of hours, or until he could gracefully make an exit, whichever came first.

The big, well-lighted space was filled almost to capacity. Women milled and chatted, men gathered in the corners to discuss the latest football standings, children darted between legs, making as much noise as possible.

Kane spotted his Aunt Mildred at one of the long serving tables, firmly directing the women assisting her. Johnnie Mae, plump and visibly content in a new, red dress, stood a few feet away, cooing over Sam and Twyla Denton's new baby, which Kane had delivered only three weeks ago. Marvin Hawkins sat in a folding chair to the right of the doorway, looking pretty good, considering that he was still recovering from the massive stroke he'd suffered several months back.

Looking around in search of his mother, Kane smiled, waved and returned greetings, already feeling a bit guilty that he'd been so reluctant to attend this gathering. After all, these were his friends, his neighbors, his patients. His family.

Despite his occasional bouts of exhaustion-induced complaining, he wouldn't trade the love in this room for a cushy, chief of staff position at the finest, most impressive hospital in the nation. That was exactly why his engagement to Cathy Pearson had come to a painful, unpleasant ending.

A friendly voice behind him broke into that flash of uncomfortable memory. "Why, hello, Kane. Glad you could make it tonight."

Kane turned to smile at the diminutive, but distinguished-looking minister who'd greeted him. Brother Curtis Wimple had been the pastor of this church since Kane was a boy. He'd even baptized Kane, who, at fourteen, had already towered nearly a foot taller than the minister—a sight that had caused some amusement among the congregation when Kane bent down to allow the preacher to dunk him backward in the baptistery behind the choir loft.

Eighteen years later it had been Kane who'd saved Brother Curtis's life, when the aging pastor nearly cut off his leg with a chain saw, while trimming tree limbs for an ailing church member. Brother Curtis still walked with a marked limp, though neither he nor his grateful family ever complained about the relatively minor result of what could have been a devastating tragedy.

"Hi, Brother Curtis. Nice turnout tonight."

Brother Curtis beamed, as if taking full credit for the social's success. "Yes, it is, isn't it? We even have a famous author joining us this evening. The ladies are all quite excited."

Kane stiffened. "Alex is here?"

He'd spent every spare moment during the day wondering about her, restraining himself from calling to check on her yet again. Why couldn't he seem to get her off his mind?

He couldn't help remembering the way she'd looked when he'd seen her in the wee hours of the morning, after finding himself unable to go back to bed without making sure she was all right. Soft and vulnerable in sleep, her smooth, tanned face had been decidedly appealing, despite the bruises from her accident. He was used to seeing people who looked vulnerable, of course, but he'd never experienced quite the same pull he'd felt when he'd gazed at Alexandra Bennett and she had smiled sleepily back.

Maybe it was the way she'd appeared out of the storm. She'd seemed so small and lost and bedraggled that his notoriously compassionate heart had been touched. Or maybe it had been the way she'd felt in his arms, as he'd carried her to the bedroom after she'd fainted. But whatever it was, he'd written it off as a passing attraction and told himself it was over, that she had already returned to her own life. He certainly hadn't expected to see her tonight, at the church social!

Brother Curtis nodded. "You've met her, then?"

"Uh . . . yes. I treated her after her accident yesterday."

"I see. Well, since she's going to be staying with your mother for a few weeks, Dottie asked her if she'd like to join us this evening. I understand Ms. Bennett's considering Andersenville as a setting for her next mystery."

Kane deliberately closed his mouth. Alex would be living next door to him? For several weeks? However had *that* come about?

He turned his head, seeking a glimpse of either the author or his mother. "Have you seen . . . ?"

The words died in his throat when the crowd suddenly parted; he saw the woman who'd been at the center of an avid group of admirers. Kane felt his breath catch somewhere deep in his chest.

Alex had appealed to him when she'd been injured and rumpled, her eyes shadowed with pain and heavy with exhaustion. Now he saw her with her near-black hair glossy and stylishly brushed, her dark chocolate eyes clear and alert, her slender curves emphasized by a beautifully tailored, silk dress. Neither the bandage at her temple nor the purple bruise on her cheek detracted from the image of a striking, self-confident, undeniably sexy woman.

He wasn't sure what he said to Brother Curtis, though he was certain he'd spoken. The next thing he knew he was moving, drawn as if by an invisible cord to the woman who'd just glanced up and seen him; her dark eyes grew wide as their gazes clashed across the room. Was he imagining things? Did those expressive eyes of hers mirror the same, physical awareness he felt at seeing her again so unexpectedly?

He'd almost made it to the spot where she stood when someone stepped in front of him. Dragging his attention away from Alex, he realized that Melanie Chastain was smiling at him, obviously expecting him to say something. She looked beautiful, as always, in a trim-cut, blue dress that set off her wide blue eyes and creamy complexion. But his pulse didn't go into a crazy rhythm when he saw her, as it had only moments before when he'd spotted Alex.

He forced a smile. "Hello, Melanie. You look very nice this evening."

She returned the smile without conceit or artifice. "Thank you, Kane. Grandmother wanted me to bring you over to say hello."

Kane glanced at the corner where Pearl Chastain sat, watching him with a group of friends from her Sunday School class. "I'd be delighted," he assured Melanie gallantly, taking her arm to accompany her.

He couldn't resist one quick glance over his shoulder.

Alex had turned away, her attention already claimed by another friend of his mother's.

4

ALEX TRIED to analyze her feelings. Melanie Chastain had waylaid Kane when he'd obviously been on his way to talk to her, instead. In one sense she was relieved. When she'd looked up and found Kane watching her she'd found herself—well, mesmerized.

So much for her assurances to herself that the attraction she'd felt for him from the beginning had diminished during the hours that had passed since she'd last seen him.

Yet, as nervous and self-conscious as her reactions to him made her, she couldn't help being a bit disappointed that Melanie had sidetracked him. There'd been something in his expression when his eyes had met hers . . . something as alluring as it was disturbing.

"Well, darn," Dottie muttered, glaring across the room.

Alex had been chatting with a local schoolteacher, who'd already asked her to speak to tenth-grade English students while she was staying in Andersenville. Since she always enjoyed speaking to young people, Alex had willingly agreed. But Dottie's low exclamation distracted her from those plans. "What's wrong, Dottie?"

Dottie shook her head and managed a weak smile. "Oh, nothing, really. I was just feeling sorry for poor Kane."

Alex looked across the room to the spot where Kane stood, surrounded by a group of women of all ages, Melanie close to his side as the others apparently competed for his attention.

Like a medieval prince holding court, Alex thought with a mental sniff of disdain. "Poor Kane?" she repeated skeptically.

Dottie nodded. "Yes. I really coerced him into being here tonight. I'm always proud to show him off, but these social things are so trying for him."

"Yes, poor Kane," the schoolteacher, Emily Hatcher, agreed sympathetically. "Everyone thinks having a doctor at a social occasion signifies an opportunity to receive free medical advice. He's probably being bombarded with symptoms at this very moment."

Chewing her lower lip, Alex looked back at the group with a new perspective. She could see now that Kane looked harried, rather than indulgent, as the others crowded ever closer to him, all seeming to speak at once. He was smiling politely, but his smile was strained around the edges. Far different from the relaxed, easy grin he'd given Alex in the middle of the night.

Despite her better judgment, she felt a bit sorry for him, herself. "Why doesn't he simply tell everyone that he's off duty, and if they have real symptoms, they should make an appointment to see him at his office?"

Both Dottie and Emily looked at Alex as though she'd suggested Kane sprout wings and fly. "Oh, he could never do that," Dottie protested. "Kane's much too polite."

"Tender-hearted," Emily agreed. "Such a sweet-natured young man."

Since Emily couldn't have been more than five years older than Kane, Alex had to forcibly repress a giggle. She glanced at him again. So Kane had a problem standing up for himself where his subjects—er, patients—were concerned, did he? How come perfect Melanie wasn't doing something to help him out, rather than just standing there, looking gorgeous?

Alex didn't realize Mildred had approached until she heard her characteristic snort of disgust.

"Just look at that," Mildred grumbled, arms crossed over her thin chest as she glared at the crowd surrounding her nephew. "Can't leave the boy alone for a minute, can they? Jennie Harrison hasn't stopped bending his ear for the past five minutes. Probably describing every pain she's had for the last six months or more. He hasn't even had a chance to speak to Melanie, and she's been standing there so patiently."

Too patiently, as far as Alex was concerned. She turned to Dottie with sudden determination. "Have I met everyone in that group?"

Dottie began to smile. "Why, no, Alex. Come along, I'll introduce you."

Mildred started to say something, but Dottie didn't give her a chance to interrupt; she swept Alex across the room, looking surprisingly daunting for such a tiny woman. Alex was aware that Mildred was following them, though Dottie didn't slow down to wait for her sister.

"Hello, Kane," Dottie said, catching her son's hand. "I'm so glad you found time to join us this evening."

"Hi, Mom," Kane said with visible relief, bending to kiss her cheek.

Only Alex, standing close to Dottie, heard him whisper, "You owe me for this, Mother." She smothered a laugh when he glanced over his mother's head to look at her.

"Hello, Doctor Lovell," she greeted him with a bland smile.

"Ms. Bennett," he returned gravely, mocking her formality. "And how is your head this evening?"

"Fine, thank you," she replied, making sure her reply could be clearly heard by the group surrounding them. "But you're off duty. I'm sure you're looking forward to relaxing with your friends this evening, rather than discussing medical business.

"After all," she added cheerfully, "even a doctor deserves a few hours away from the job, doesn't he?" She directed a smiling glance around them as she spoke, including everyone in the question.

Looking rather sheepish, the others immediately nodded in fervent agreement, none of them quite able to meet Kane's eyes.

Dottie stepped gracefully into the ensuing silence. "Has everyone met my guest this evening? This is Alexandra Bennett, the best-selling mystery author. She'll be staying with me for the next few weeks while she researches her next book."

"Please call me Alex," Alex added, giving her best, public-relations smile. "I'm very pleased to be here. Everyone has been so welcoming to me."

As though to reinforce her praise, the others immediately greeted her with warm enthusiasm, showering her with compliments and questions about her work, offering assistance with research, introducing themselves in a cacophony of names and tidbits of personal information.

Alex fielded the attention graciously, calling on past experience with book signings and gatherings of avid, aspiring writers. She noticed that Dottie gave Mildred a rather taunting smile that Mildred returned with a scowl, but Alex was too busy shaking hands and trying to memorize names to guess at what was going on between the sisters.

Melanie quickly took advantage of the distraction Alex had provided. "You must be hungry, Kane," she murmured, taking his arm. "The ladies have provided a wonderful buffet."

"Yes, Melanie, why don't you help Kane fix his plate?" Mildred urged throwing a satisfied look at her sister. "Come along. I'll get you a glass of tea, Kane."

"Hmm," Dottie grumbled, just loudly enough for Alex to hear. "That boy's perfectly capable of preparing his own plate."

But again, Alex was too busy answering questions to reply. *Just as well* she thought, holding on to her smile with an effort.

THE MEMBERS of the First Baptist Church of Andersenville, Alex learned during the next two hours, were a gregarious, closely knit, intensely curious bunch. Alex suspected that they spent a great deal of time discussing each other's personal lives. She believed just as strongly that there was little they wouldn't do for someone in need.

They were real people with real flaws and virtues. Not perfect, but then Alex had always found perfection rather dull. She was having a very nice time at the social, despite her bewilderingly ambiguous feelings toward Kane Lovell.

She had no further chance to speak to Kane until the social was drawing to an end. Alex looked up from a friendly chat with the kind-eyed, aging minister to find Dottie bearing down on them with Kane in tow. Alex was grateful that she'd never been the type to blush easily; had she been, she suspected her cheeks would have warmed then. Kane had been in her mind, even as she'd looked up to find him so close.

"So, what do you think of our visiting celebrity, Brother Curtis?" Dottie asked teasingly.

The minister smiled. "I was just telling Alex that I've always had a yen to write, myself. I've toyed for years with a humorous story about a rural minister, perhaps using some of the experiences I've had with this congregation. Of course, I know Andy Griffith starred in an old movie based on a similar story, but I like to think that I could bring a fresh approach to my own tale."

"You know what they say, Pastor Wimple," Alex told him with a grin. "There are only seven original plots, and Shakespeare used them all. The rest of us have to settle with trying to find a fresh approach. You should write your book. It sounds like a lot of fun."

"Thank you," he said, looking pleased. "Perhaps I will."

Dottie tapped Alex's shoulder. "Alex, Kane just told me that he's leaving. Since I'm staying for a while to help with the cleanup, I thought you'd like him to give you a lift home."

"It's not as if it would be out of my way," Kane added with a smile. "Are you ready to go, Alex?"

She wondered if it would be wiser to decline, to offer to help Dottie. Her reactions to Kane were so strong, so confusing. But then, if Alex hadn't learned to take a few chances along the way, she never would have gotten her first book published. "Yes, I'm ready."

Kane gestured toward the door. "Then shall we go?"

Alex took her leave of the minister and then Dottie, eyeing the older woman's decidedly smug smile for a moment before turning to accompany Kane out of the church. She was very careful not to look Melanie's way as she left, though she suspected that Melanie was watching Kane and herself as intently as everyone else seemed to be.

She stifled a sigh. It wasn't hard to guess who'd be the primary subject of conversation for the ladies of the First Baptist Church's cleanup committee.

ALEX STRAPPED HERSELF into the passenger seat of Kane's car, intensely aware of him as he fumbled with his own seat belt, his hand only inches from hers. He gave her a fleeting smile and started the engine, while Alex had to make a conscious effort to restart her breathing. How could he *do* that with nothing more than a smile? she wondered in utter bewilderment.

"I suppose you're glad to escape," Kane commented, guiding his car out of the church parking lot.

Distracted from her analysis of her unprecedented physical reaction to this man, she turned to him with a question. "To escape what?"

He jerked his chin to indicate the church they were leaving behind. "The social. Must be a lot different from the glamorous parties you're accustomed to in Chicago."

She tilted her head, studying him curiously. "What makes you think I'm accustomed to glamorous parties?"

"Well, aren't you?"

"Not particularly. My parents were both very serious, rather reclusive university professors and historians. I was a legal secretary before I quit to write full-time. Hardly a jet-setter background."

Kane raised an eyebrow. "Oh. Well, still, you're a famous author now. You must do a lot of socializing."

She was rather enjoying having the upper hand over him—for once. "If I did a lot of socializing, I wouldn't get much writing done, would I?" she asked sweetly.

"Well, er . . ."

"Writing is a lonely business, Kane. I spend an average of eight hours a day in my apartment, shut in the spare bedroom I've converted to an office. I communicate with my agent and publishers mostly by telephone or fax machine and go on publicity tours or book signings only when it seems absolutely necessary, since I find those things so stressful and exhausting. As for the church social—I enjoyed that more than I have any 'glamorous party' I've attended in a very long time. Does that surprise you?"

"Yes," he admitted. "I would have thought a writer's life was more . . . well, exotic."

"A lot of people think that," she replied. "The truth is, we're just ordinary people with vivid imaginations.

Writing is a job—a great job, I'll admit, and one I wouldn't trade for any other—but it involves long hours of hard work if one wants to be successful at it. Granted, my career isn't life-and-death crucial, the way yours is, but . . ."

Kane interrupted with a laugh and one upraised hand. "All right, you've made your point. You're a career woman, not a party animal."

"Exactly." She crossed her arms in a gesture of satisfaction.

He hesitated a moment, then asked carefully, "Am I going to set you off again if I ask whether you were gathering research for your book tonight? I mean, I know some of the people you met were eccentric—like any small town, we have our share—but they're good people. I wouldn't want you to embarrass them, or the town in general, in your book, if you're planning to lampoon small, Southern towns the way so many writers take such pleasure in doing."

Alex took a very deep breath and counted to ten. Twice. "Yes," she said, after practicing that calming exercise. "You're going to 'set me off again.' I realize you feel a certain protectiveness toward your loyal subjects, but I don't believe I've given you any reason to think I'd embarrass those very nice people by 'lampooning' them in my book.

"My purpose in writing is to provide entertainment and to stimulate imaginations. I don't do hatchet jobs and I don't intentionally target any group for mockery or degradation. You'd know that if you'd ever read anything I've written, rather than basing your arrogant, unfounded accusations on what some other writers may have done in other books!"

"Whew!" Kane whistled. He had the grace to look sheepish when he slanted her a sideways look. "I really *did* hit a nerve, didn't I? I'm sorry, Alex. You're right, I shouldn't judge your work without having read it. I was just expressing an opinion. And what do you mean, my 'loyal subjects'? Shouldn't you have said my friends?"

Refusing to be appeased that easily, she glared out the side window to avoid looking at his quizzical smile. "Come on, Kane. Everyone knows how a small-town doctor is revered and respected. Look at the way you were catered to tonight. Hell, you hold those people's very lives in your hands. It's no wonder you tend to consider it your full-time responsibility to watch out for them!"

"*Now* who's generalizing?" Kane demanded. "And don't you think you're overstating things just a bit? I don't . . ."

But Alex wasn't listening. A glimpse of something black-and-white down a secluded-looking lane leading off the highway made her sit up straighter. "The cow!"

"Cow?" Kane repeated, struggling to follow the sudden change of subject. "What cow?"

"It was walking down that little road we just passed," Alex replied, craning her neck to look behind them, wincing as her still-sore neck muscles protested. "I'm sure it's the same one that caused my accident last night. Shouldn't we do something before it wanders back onto the highway and causes another one?"

Kane applied the brakes, pulling to the side of the road. "I suppose it wouldn't hurt to check it out," he said, looking behind him before throwing the car into reverse and backing up.

She remained silent as Kane turned into the heavily shadowed, unlighted lane, the headlamps cutting broad swaths into the darkness ahead. Alex saw deep ruts in the road, heavy brush lining the ditches, and the glitter of what might be water at the far end of the road...but no cow.

"I'm sure I saw it," she fretted, looking from side to side as Kane carefully navigated the rough road. "The moonlight reflected off the white patches on its back. It was walking straight ahead."

"There's a little pond at the end of this road. Maybe it's thirsty."

Minutes later, Kane parked the car beside the pond and cut the engine. He waited patiently while Alex squirmed in her seat to look all around them. "Well?" he said when she finally gave a grumble of disgust and slumped back into the seat.

"I don't see it," she admitted. "But it *was* there, Kane."

He shrugged. "Probably ran into the woods when we came along," he suggested. "Someone will most likely catch it tomorrow. Don't worry about it."

Alex sighed and shook her head. "I'm just frustrated that so far I'm the only one who has seen it. It's enough to make a person start questioning her vision."

"Und haf you had zeese bovine hallucinations often, Mees Bennett?" Kane teased in a terrible, mock-Freudian accent.

She couldn't help laughing. "No, Dr. Lovell. Only since I landed in Oz yesterday."

He caught one of her curls between two fingers and tugged idly at it. "You were expecting flying monkeys, perhaps?"

Her breath caught somewhere in the back of her throat as she realized again just how close he sat in the confines of the small car. "Mmm...what was the question again?" she asked, struggling to follow the teasing.

He held her gaze with his, his own smile fading. "I forgot," he murmured, dropping the curl to slide his fingers into the hair at the back of her head. "Alex..."

She didn't stop to think as she raised her parted lips to his. Without breaking eye contact, Kane lowered his head, paused only a breath away, then slowly brushed his mouth over hers. Alex could have groaned in frustration when he drew back after only that brief, wholly unsatisfying contact.

His expression shuttered, Kane drew his hand from her hair and started the car. "Let's just consider that an apology for my nasty, suspicious nature, shall we?" he suggested lightly.

Alex looked at her tightly clasped hands. "Apology accepted," she answered, much more casually than she felt.

"Good."

They said little more during the brief ride home. Kane pulled into his mother's driveway. "I'll walk you to the door."

"No, that's not necessary. Dottie gave me a key. Thanks for the ride home, Kane. I'll . . . be seeing you around."

"Yes. Good night, Alex."

"Good night, Kane." She was out of the car before he could say anything else, hurrying toward the front door as though . . . as though all the cows of hell were pursuing her, she thought with a futile attempt at humor.

She didn't relax until she was safely inside her temporary bedroom, sitting on the edge of her bed with her face hidden in her hands. Only then did she allow herself to relive a kiss that had been one of the most staggering experiences of her life, despite its brevity.

"What is going on here?" she asked wearily, carefully brushing her fingers over the neat bandage at her temple. "What have you gotten yourself into *now*, Alexandra?"

"OKAY, so she handled herself well at the church social," Mildred conceded grudgingly as she drove her housemates home later that evening. "It's not as though that proves anything, really. After all, a famous author is used to mingling and socializing. Doesn't mean she's right for Kane."

"You were the one who said she wouldn't fit in with our friends and neighbors," Dottie pointed out archly. "She had them eating out of her hand before the evening was over. And did you see the way she took the pressure off Kane by pointing out that he deserved some time away from work? And she managed it so tactfully, she didn't offend anyone, not even Jennie."

"That was sweet of her," Johnnie Mae seconded. "Kane needs someone who can do that for him. Of course, after being president of the PTA for the past two years, Connie Travers is very good at diplomacy, as well. I really think the two of you should give her a bit more consideration."

"That youngest kid of hers cried all evening," Mildred pointed out. "Who'd wish that on poor Kane?"

Johnnie Mae immediately became defensive. "Well, one of the bigger children stepped on little Joey's foot. He couldn't help that. Usually Connie's children are perfectly behaved!"

"We're discussing Alex, remember?" Dottie folded her hands in her lap. "I think something serious could develop between Kane and Alex. The way he looked at her . . . well, it made my pulse race."

Mildred shook her head. "You've demonstrated she's good at a party. Kane needs someone who's good at a lot more than that. Someone who's capable of handling a real emergency, for example. Just think of all the situations a doctor's wife could find herself in. What good would a party girl be in a medical emergency? Look at the way Melanie helped out when Alex showed up, bleeding and fainting. Now *that's* the way a doctor's wife responds!"

"I'm not sure I'd call Alex a party girl," Johnnie Mae murmured thoughtfully.

"Nor would I," Dottie agreed heatedly. "And I have a feeling she'd handle herself just fine in a medical emergency! She's a levelheaded, intelligent young woman, who seems capable of doing anything she puts her mind to. I'm certain she would make you eat those words, Mildred."

Johnnie Mae smiled wryly. "At least this is one test the two of you can't arrange. Not even you two would cause a true medical emergency just to see how Alex responds."

"And, of course, I wouldn't wish something like that to happen," Dottie said. "But if it did . . ."

"If it did, you'd see that I'm right about Alex." Mildred spoke with her usual certainty.

Johnnie Mae sighed deeply as the argument escalated. "This one is a waste of breath," she muttered. "Who can know for sure how anyone would react to a true emergency?"

ALEX SPENT the next two days working, researching the town and its history, spending hours in her room with her notepads, outlines and computer. It wasn't that she was avoiding Kane, she assured herself, it was simply that she'd been too busy to waste time thinking about him or watching for him. Besides, if she *was* avoiding him, then Kane was apparently avoiding her just as diligently; even his mother had commented that he'd certainly made himself scarce since the church social.

She was touched that the townspeople were so co-operative—everyone, from the farmer who gave her a lengthy tour of his operation and an overview of rural farm life, to the local librarian, who gave her invaluable assistance in finding information about the area from old books and documents. What a pleasant town Andersenville had turned out to be!

On her second day out, she stopped impulsively at an inviting-looking diner on Main Street, intending to have a light meal and soak up a bit more local atmosphere.

"You're that writer lady, aren't you?" asked the skinny, blushing young man who handed her a menu and stood poised to take her order.

"Why, yes," Alex answered with a smile, judging him to be about seventeen. "I'm Alex Bennett. How did you know?"

"I saw you at the church social the other night," he admitted. "I wanted to meet you then, but I never got a chance. I'm Tommy Kelley. My dad owns this diner."

"It's very nice to meet you, Tommy."

"You, too, Ms. Bennett. You see . . ." Tommy's blush deepened noticeably. "I want to be a writer, too," he confessed, shuffling his feet self-consciously.

Alex had long since stopped being surprised at the number of people who told her they dreamed of being published. It was a fairly common reaction when people found out what she did for a living. She nodded encouragingly. "What do you write?"

"Science fiction," he answered promptly. "My high school teachers all tell me I have real talent. I'm going to college next year. Ole Miss. I've got a scholarship."

"Congratulations. How long have you been writing?"

"Ever since I could hold a pencil," Tommy replied ruefully. "When all the other guys were out throwing baseballs and shooting baskets, I was sitting in my room with notebooks and reference books. They used to make fun of me sometimes."

"They won't make fun when they see your name on the cover of a book," Alex assured him.

Tommy's grin stretched almost ear to ear, and Alex knew she'd just won another fan. She ordered a salad and a glass of iced tea, then promised Tommy she'd be glad to answer any questions he might have about the publishing business, sometime when he wasn't working at the diner. He thanked her fervently before hurrying away with her order.

By the time Alex returned to her temporary home later that afternoon, she was tired, but quite satisfied with her progress. She'd made several friends around the town, learned a great deal about farm life, and was moving along with the story line that was developing in her notes. And all without thinking about Kane Lovell...well, no more than once every hour or so, she amended wryly.

She filled her arms with the books and notebooks from the passenger seat, staggering a bit under the weight. Concentrating on balancing the stack as she took a step toward the house, she nearly screamed when two large, tanned hands suddenly appeared to relieve her of part of her burden.

"What are you trying to do, end up in traction?" Kane scolded, frowning at Alex as he towered over her. "These books are entirely too heavy to carry in one load."

Alex sighed gustily. "I'm perfectly capable of taking care of myself, Dr. Lovell."

"Right," he grunted, obviously not convinced. "Come on, I'll help you get these inside. Is there anything else?"

"No, that's all," she told him grudgingly.

The stack of books tucked into one arm, Kane gestured gravely with his free hand. "After you," he said, his manner mockingly formal.

Alex glared at him for a moment, then turned and stalked toward the house, her chin high. This had to be one of the most bossy, infuriating men she'd ever met!

Too bad he was also the most fascinating.

5

As THOUGH she'd been watching for their arrival, Dottie threw open the front door, just as Alex and Kane stepped onto the porch. "Goodness, what's all this?" she asked, eyeing the stacks of books and notebooks they carried.

"Research," Alex replied.

"Heavy," Kane added.

Dottie smiled. "I hope you're both hungry. I've made something special for dinner this evening. It should be ready in another half hour or so."

"What's the occasion?" Kane asked over his shoulder, following Alex down the hall.

"Oh, I just felt like trying something new," Dottie called back cheerfully. "You kids take your time. I'll be in the kitchen if you need me."

"Kids?" Alex repeated, dumping her things onto the bed. "It's been awhile since I've been called a kid."

Kane chuckled, setting the books on a corner of the desk. "Compared to Mom and Aunt Mildred and Johnnie Mae, you are a kid," he pointed out.

"I'll be thirty in a few weeks."

He laughed at her morose tone. "It's not that bad, surely. I'll be thirty-four in a couple of months."

She smiled wryly. "I know, it's only a state of mind. But I'll confess I'm not looking forward to my birthday."

"I assure you, you don't look a day over twenty-nine," Kane teased gravely.

"Oh, thanks so much." She flinched when he reached out to her. "What are you doing?"

Looking surprised, he stood still, his hand out-stretched. "I was just going to have a look at those stitches. Any problem with that?"

Feeling foolish, Alex managed a stilted laugh and shook her head. "Sorry. You startled me."

He stepped closer, carefully easing the bandage away from her skin. Alex kept her eyes trained sternly on the top button of his white shirt. "Have you had any pain?" Kane asked matter-of-factly.

"Not particularly," Alex replied, hoping her own voice sounded as normal. "It's still rather sore, but I suppose that's to be expected."

"Yes." He prodded gently, his fingers barely brushing the still-puffy skin around the injury. "Does that hurt?"

"No," she answered in little more than a whisper, her hands clenching behind her. He was so close. So big. So warm. Utterly virile and breathtakingly gorgeous.

"I'd say you were healing nicely."

"Oh. That's—that's good to hear." She moistened her lips, which had suddenly gone dry.

"Come by the clinic Monday, and I'll take the stitches out. You can leave the bandage off, if you like," he added without stepping back. "It's not necessary, un-less you just want to cover the stitches for cosmetic reasons."

"I don't suppose the stitches look any worse than the bandage." Alex tried to sound matter-of-fact, though it was one of the hardest things she'd ever done. The top two buttons of his shirt were undone, exposing his throat and a hint of dark hair beneath. The top of her head came just to his chin, putting her at eye level with the pulse that throbbed visibly, intriguingly in the hollow of his throat.

She held her breath as she waited for him to move away, hoping her suddenly clouded mind would clear when he wasn't standing quite so close. But he didn't move, and she looked up at him warily. He met her gaze with his own, and a ripple of awareness went through her in response to the heat she saw in his eyes.

His fingertips still rested lightly against her cheek. She felt a tremor there. Hers—or his?

"Kane?" she whispered, searching his face for some clue to what he was feeling.

He lowered his head. Closing her eyes, she rose to meet him.

"Alex?"

The single word, called from the hallway beyond the open bedroom door, pulled Alex away from Kane as effectively as an angry hand. Swallowing a gasp, she whirled to face the doorway, where Mildred appeared a moment later.

"Oh, there you are," Mildred said, her sharp gaze going quickly from Alex to Kane. "I hope I'm not interrupting anything," she added rather disapprovingly.

"Of course not," Alex assured her with a bright, utterly false smile. "Kane was just checking my stitches."

"Oh." Mildred's frown faded a bit. She held out a scrap of yellow notepaper. "You had a couple of telephone messages this afternoon. One's from your insurance agent. The other's from your boyfriend in Chicago," she added clearly. "He seemed very disappointed that you weren't here when he called."

Alex swallowed. "Thank you, Mildred. I appreciate your taking the messages for me. I hope it wasn't an inconvenience."

"Not at all," the older woman assured her, then looked to her nephew. "You're staying for dinner, Kane?"

"Yes."

Alex eyed him from beneath her lashes as he spoke. Whatever she'd seen in his expression before was gone now, his jaw set in stern, unrevealing lines.

"Why don't I get you something to drink before dinner?" Mildred suggested, waiting for him to accompany her from the room. "You'd probably like to put your feet up for a few minutes while Dottie's finishing in the kitchen."

"That sounds nice, Aunt Mildred." Kane took a step toward her, then glanced at Alex. "Coming?"

"I'd like to freshen up a bit," she answered, turning her fake smile toward him. "I'll be along in a few minutes."

Kane nodded and walked out without looking back, followed closely by his aunt. Alex stared after him for several long, tense moments, heedless of the scrap of paper crumpled in her hand.

He would have kissed her, had Mildred not appeared. But would he have *really* kissed her this time? Or would it have been another fleeting brush of lips that left her aching for more?

Picturing the look in his eyes as they'd hovered only inches from her own, she shivered, knowing it would definitely have been a real kiss. And if that brief kiss in his car, Wednesday night, had shaken her to her toenails, what would a *real* kiss have done to her?

She didn't know if she was more relieved or disappointed that she hadn't had the opportunity to find out.

It would be best for everyone concerned, of course, if Alex stayed well away from Kane Lovell during her remaining time in Andersenville. Whatever chemistry or attraction existed between them, it could only lead to trouble if they encouraged it. Alex had a life in Chicago, Kane was firmly established here. His aunt, at least, seemed well aware that the two of them were all wrong for each other. Mildred couldn't have expressed her feelings more clearly if she'd said them flat out.

"Forget him. Alexandra," she ordered herself, though she kept her voice quiet. "You're only asking for trouble if you aren't careful."

But her cheek still tingled from the touch of his fingers hours ago. And no other man had ever made her tingle.

"Dammit," she muttered and took a deep breath, preparing herself for another evening with Kane.

ALEX AND KANE SAID LITTLE directly to each other during dinner, letting Dottie, Mildred and Johnnie Mae carry the conversation. Alex wondered if Kane was as intensely aware of her during the meal as she was of him, despite the care they took to avoid each other's eyes.

Though her feelings for Kane were terribly mixed, Alex couldn't help but be touched by the way he treated his hostesses. It was obvious that he was very close to his mother, but he seemed almost as fond of his acerbic Aunt Mildred and funny, scatterbrained Johnnie Mae. Not many men his age would have been as patient with the ladies' blunt comments and blatantly prying questions about his personal affairs.

Mildred, in particular, seemed compelled to bring up Melanie's name in every other sentence. Alex noted that Kane gently, but firmly, changed the subject each time, much to her relief.

"Oh, Kane, I wonder if you'd look at Cujo before you leave," Johnnie Mae said just as they were finishing dessert. "I'm a little worried about him."

"Cujo?" Kane repeated, looking up with a frown.

"Jason's pet tarantula," she reminded him. "I've been keeping it for him while he's off on that college trip."

Alex was amused to note that Kane paled just noticeably beneath his tan. "Uh . . . what do you want me to do with it, Johnnie Mae?" he asked cautiously. "I really don't know much about . . . er . . . animals."

"Gee, Kane," Alex couldn't resist saying, "all you have to do is have it stick out its tongue and say 'Ahh.'"

He glared at her. "Maybe if I could find its mouth," he muttered.

"It may take you a while to test its reflexes," she added mischievously. "Just think of all the knees you'd have to tap."

Dottie giggled. "And how would you know where to take its blood pressure?" she asked, joining in the silliness. "How would you know what was an arm and what was a leg?"

Mildred was not amused. "Why couldn't Jason have a dog for a pet, like everyone else? That boy always has been peculiar."

Johnnie Mae sat up. "My nephew is *not* peculiar!" she exclaimed defensively. " He's just . . . creative."

Alex bit her lip against a smile.

Looking worried again, Johnnie Mae turned back to Kane. "I'm not asking you to examine the thing, of course, Kane. It's just that . . . well, I thought it was sleeping, but it hasn't moved in two days. I'm terribly afraid that it's . . . well, dead."

The teasing ended abruptly. "Uh-oh," Dottie murmured.

Johnnie Mae nodded woefully. "I know. Jason's so fond of the thing. I don't know how I'd tell him if—"

"Maybe it *is* sleeping," Alex suggested hopefully. "Maybe tar—" She couldn't help shuddering as she said the awful word. "—tarantulas go into hibernation when they don't eat for a few days."

"Oh, it's eaten," Johnnie Mae assured them. "I fed it some crickets. It seemed to enjoy them."

"Crickets?" Kane asked with a sudden frown. "Where'd you get them?"

"Why, from under the house. You know how much trouble we've been having with the darn things lately. I figured I'd get rid of a few of them, at least."

"Oh, dear," Dottie said, covering her mouth with one tiny hand.

"Johnnie Mae, I called an exterminator earlier this week," Kane explained gently. "He sprayed under the house to help get rid of those crickets."

Johnnie Mae's eyes grew round. "You mean, those crickets may have been . . ."

"Poisoned," Mildred said with a crack of laughter. "Now *there*'s an interesting murder weapon for one of your books, Alex."

Dottie glared at her sister. "Honestly, Mildred."

"Oh, goodness. Oh, heavens!" Johnnie Mae wrung her hands in distress.

Kane sighed and pushed his chair away from the table. "Come on, Johnnie Mae. I'll take a look at it for you."

Because Johnnie Mae looked so upset, Alex resisted an impulse to suggest that Kane try mouth-to-mouth resuscitation, if all else failed.

Returning to the dining room, the doctor soberly pronounced the patient dead. "I'm afraid there's nothing else we can do," he added. "Do you want me to dispose of it for you, Johnnie Mae?"

"Oh, goodness, no," Johnnie Mae said immediately. "I'd better wait and let Jason decide what to do with it. He may want to have it mounted or something."

Alex thought she might be sick.

Kane didn't linger for long after that. He kissed the older ladies' cheeks as he left, giving Alex a rather stilted smile and a formal good-night.

Alex spent a very restless night, unable to forget the look in Kane's eyes as he'd leaned toward her when they were alone in her room, unable to stop wondering what the kiss might have been like. What he might have said afterward.

A BOYFRIEND IN CHICAGO. Kane shoved a hand through his hair and glared out the kitchen window at the spot where a light glowed, in Alex's bedroom, the only light on in his mother's house in the middle of the night. He should have known, he thought grimly. Though he might have been wrong about Alex living a frivolous, party-filled life in Chicago, he should have guessed that a woman like her would be involved with someone, no matter how hard she claimed to work.

He wondered why she hadn't mentioned the guy. He wondered if she lived with him. He wondered if she was in love with him.

He wondered how hard it would be to take her away from him.

"Dammit!" he muttered, slamming a hand, palm down, upon the kitchen counter. The sharp sound echoed through the empty house. What was he doing, standing here in the middle of the night, staring longingly at Alex's window like some love-struck adolescent? Hadn't he learned anything at all from his fiasco of an engagement to Cathy? Was he that much of a masochist to be falling again for a woman who could never fit into his life?

It wasn't as if he had no alternatives, he reminded himself sternly. All he had to do was pick up the phone, and he could arrange a date with any one of several attractive, available—and agreeable—women. Women who'd been raised in Andersenville, who wanted nothing more than to lead a quiet, contented life here, raise families here, which was what Kane wanted, as well.

The problem was that none of those women interested him at the moment as much as the dark-haired, dark-eyed, temperamental writer, sitting, even now, in his mother's spare bedroom.

Why was she still awake? Was she working? Reading? Thinking of him?

"You're dreaming, Lovell," he grumbled, shaking his head in self-disgust.

She was all wrong for him. He wanted someone comfortable, someone adaptable, someone who wouldn't mind taking second place at times to the demands of his career. Something told him Alexandra Bennett didn't care for taking second place to anything or anyone. And the feelings she roused in him were anything but comfortable.

He wanted her. Had, perhaps, from the first moment he'd seen her. He just didn't know what the hell he was going to do about it.

Alexandra Bennett was a potential heartache in a petite, brunette package. And Kane Lovell had come too far in his life to risk that kind of pain again.

Maybe he should give Melanie Chastain a call sometime. She, of course, much more closely resembled the woman Kane had been looking for during the past couple of years. His Aunt Mildred had hinted broadly enough that Melanie wouldn't be averse to going out with him. He liked Melanie, and wanted to believe he could find himself liking her even more, if he spent more time with her. She seemed so much more suited to him, to the plans he'd made....

Too bad the thought of Melanie didn't make his teeth ache, he thought, casting one more resentful glance toward Alex's window. He turned and stalked through the house to his lonely bed.

AFTER A RESTLESS, dream-filled night, Alex gave up trying to sleep and crawled out of bed early Saturday morning, taking care to be quiet as she dressed and headed for the kitchen. She didn't want to wake any of her housemates, if they had decided to sleep in on this nice, weekend morning.

She found Johnnie Mae sitting at the kitchen table, bent industriously over what looked like a square of plywood. "Good morning," Alex greeted the older woman, gratefully heading for the full pot of coffee she'd spotted the moment she entered the room.

"Good morning, dear. Did you sleep well?"

"Fine, thank you," Alex lied cheerfully. "How about you? I hope you didn't worry too much about . . . Oh,

God!" She stopped abruptly in midstep, sloshing hot coffee over the rim of her cup and onto her hand.

"Ouch!" Hastily switching the cup to her left hand, she examined the reddened skin on her right knuckles, relieved to note that she hadn't seriously burned herself.

"Alex, honey, are you all right?" Johnnie Mae asked in concern.

"Yes, I'm . . . Johnnie Mae, *what* are you doing?"

The older woman looked a bit sheepishly at the board on the table in front of her—at the hairy corpse that rested there. "I was just pinning Cujo's feet to this board."

Alex swallowed weakly, unable to look directly at the table. "Uh . . . you want to tell me why?"

"Well, I want to keep him for Jason, but I was afraid he'd start to smell. So I thought I'd freeze him," Johnnie Mae explained, obviously proud of her brainstorm. "I'll just finish pinning him to this board, then I'll stick him in the deep freeze in the storage room. That should work, shouldn't it?"

"I guess so," Alex agreed hesitantly, "but be sure and warn the others about it being in there."

"Oh, I will."

Alex eased toward the back door. "You know, it's such a lovely morning, I think I'll take my coffee out on the patio and watch the birds."

Johnnie Mae smiled in obvious understanding. "Yes, why don't you do that, dear? I should be finished here in a few minutes and then I'll join you."

Alex managed a smile that felt sickly, turned and all but fled outside.

HAVING SPENT most of Saturday with her research books and computer, Alex got up early again on Sunday to accompany her hostesses to church, as they'd invited her to do the night before. The church members greeted her like an old friend, making her feel warm and welcome among them. Alex sat beside Dottie in a pew close to the front. She didn't even mind too much when Melanie Chastain and her grandmother settled into the pew behind them with friendly, soft-spoken greetings.

At least she was spared having to face Kane during the morning. Dottie explained that she'd heard he'd been called to the hospital early to deliver a baby. "A doctor's life," she said ruefully, glancing at Alex as though to test her response.

Alex murmured something noncommittal and pretended to be absorbed in the church bulletin she'd been given when she entered the sanctuary.

Alex and her hostesses decided to dine out after the service. Dottie graciously extended an invitation to Pearl and Melanie to join them. They seemed delighted to accept. They ate at the diner where Alex had eaten lunch on Friday. Judging from the crowd, it was quite a popular establishment.

"Hank Kelley's father opened this place back in the forties," Dottie explained for Alex's benefit. "And it's still the best food in town. Beats those fast-food places all to pieces."

Tommy Kelley seemed delighted to see Alex again. "Hi, Miss Bennett!" he greeted her with a broad smile, ushering her to her seat with a flourish worthy of a maître d'. "I just finished reading your new book. It was great! You had me completely fooled about who the killer was."

"I'm glad to hear it," she said, slightly embarrassed by the attention he was giving her. "I was trying to keep the readers guessing."

"You sure did that," Tommy agreed with a laugh. "I thought it was the cop."

"Tommy!" A man Alex judged to be the young man's father called across the crowded room. "You've got orders waiting."

Tommy flushed. "Oops. I'll be right back to take y'all's orders," he promised, hurrying away.

"Well, Alex. It seems you have quite a fan here," Dottie commented with a smile.

"He wants to write science fiction," Alex responded. "He's a nice boy."

"We've known Tommy Kelley all his life," Johnnie Mae said. "He always has had an active imagination."

"Did you know Melanie made the dress she's wearing?" Mildred asked, seemingly out of the blue. "Melanie's quite an accomplished seamstress, isn't she, Pearl?"

Melanie blushed charmingly as her grandmother agreed that she was quite talented. Alex joined the others in complimenting Melanie on the lovely lines of her paisley silk dress. "I've never tried to sew anything," she admitted. "It always seemed so complicated."

"Grandmother taught me to sew when I was just a girl," Melanie explained. "It's not hard. It just takes practice in getting the fit right."

"Melanie even made her own gown for the senior prom," Pearl said proudly. "It was the most beautiful dress you've ever seen. Organdy and lace, with tiny little seed pearls embroidered on the bodice. She looked just like a fairy princess."

"I'm sure she did," Alex said with a tiny, silent sigh.

She allowed her attention to wander during lunch, glancing across the table at Melanie, who gave her a wry smile in response to the older women's avid gossiping. It should have been very easy not to like Melanie Chastain, Alex thought regretfully. If only Melanie hadn't been quite so darned nice!

They were just preparing to leave the restaurant when a commotion in one corner of the dining room made them stop and look around. A woman screamed; a man staggered out of his chair, one hand on his chest, and collapsed on the floor of the restaurant.

"My God, it's Zeb Cavender!" Dottie said with a horrified gasp. "Someone call an ambulance!"

Alex was already hurrying across the room, responding automatically to a situation she'd hoped never to encounter in reality. She'd learned CPR during research for her first book and had found the training so vital and fascinating that she'd taken regular refresher courses since. She'd only hoped she'd never really have to use it.

"He's having a heart attack!" Zeb's wife shrieked frantically, kneeling beside her prone husband. "Someone help him."

"Does anyone here know CPR?" another diner asked, looking as though he regretted that he didn't know the procedure, himself.

"I do." Alex responded at the same time as young Tommy Kelley, who flushed and explained quickly that he'd learned in Boy Scouts. Sensing that everyone was waiting for someone to take over, Alex dropped to her knees beside Zeb, motioning for Tommy to join her.

Zeb's lips were already turning blue, his skin was pale and clammy. Alex felt frantically for a pulse, first in his thick neck and then his wrist, but could find nothing.

As far as she could tell, he wasn't breathing. "Has someone called for an ambulance?" she asked, her stomach tightening. She realized that the man was dying right in front of her.

"Mildred is calling," Johnnie Mae answered tensely. "Alex, is he . . . ?"

Zeb's wife burst into noisy tears. Dottie wrapped her arms around the other woman, trying to soothe her.

Alex met Tommy's worried eyes. "There's no pulse and no breathing," she said, keeping her voice low. He swallowed audibly and nodded, looking determined to do whatever he could to help.

Her instructor's voice echoed in her ears. *You only have a few minutes to save someone who has stopped breathing. Every moment you wait makes recovery less likely.* "Let's start CPR," Alex said to Tommy.

He nodded. "I'll do the breathing, you handle the compressions. I don't mind giving mouth-to-mouth. I had to do it once before, when a friend almost drowned at the swimming pool."

She gave him a quick, tight smile. "That's good to hear. Okay. Five compressions, one breath. Let's get him in position."

Working as though they'd practiced for weeks, they positioned Zeb's arms and legs, then tipped his head back to clear his airway. Alex checked one more time for a pulse or any sign of breathing. When she found nothing, she knelt closer to him, quickly running her hands over his chest until she'd found the right location for her fingers.

Glancing at Tommy, she nodded and began to push smoothly against Zeb's unresponsive chest, counting as she administered the compressions. "One, one thousand. Two, one thousand. Three, one thousand. Four, one thousand. Five, breathe!"

Keeping Zeb's head tilted with one hand and his nose pinched shut with the other, Tommy blew a full breath into the older man's open mouth. Alex didn't pause, but kept the count and the compressions going. "One, one thousand. Two, one thousand . . ."

Tommy checked for a pulse when they'd been at it for perhaps a minute. He shook his head. "Nothing."

"Keep going. One, one thousand. Two, one thousand . . ." Concentrating with all her energy on the life that was slipping away beneath her hands, Alex was hardly aware of the silent crowd of onlookers surrounding them, watching with held breath and whispered prayers. She couldn't have guessed at how much time passed as she worked, holding on to her composure with a massive effort.

"Three, one thousand . . . Four, one thousand . . ."

"Okay, hold it." A white-uniformed medic dropped to his knees beside her, followed closely by another.

Alex could have wept with relief. Instead, she moved swiftly out of their way, joining the watching crowd as the medical emergency technicians bent over their patient. Long, tense, activity-filled moments later, there was a collective cheer of relief when one of the technicians announced, "I've got a pulse! Let's get him into the ambulance."

"Oh, thank God!" Zeb's wife cried, pulling herself out of Dottie's supportive arms. She followed as Zeb was wheeled briskly out of the restaurant.

"Alex, you saved Zeb's life!" Melanie said with a touch of awe. "That was wonderful. You, too, Tommy. I'm so proud of you."

Tommy flushed a bright red, shyly meeting Alex's eyes. She reached out to hug him. "*You* were wonderful," she told him. "I don't know if I could have done that without you."

"You think Zeb will make it?"

Alex didn't want to lead him on. "I don't know, Tommy. He could go into arrest again on the way to the hospital. But he has a chance."

"Thanks to the two of you," Dottie murmured, her cheeks wet with tears. She wrapped her arms around Alex's waist and hugged tightly. "Alex, you're amazing."

Alex was getting embarrassed, especially when she found herself surrounded by people wanting to shake her hand and congratulate her on her actions, all of them including Tommy in their praise. She was touched by the tribute, but relieved when Dottie finally insisted that it was time to go, to allow Alex a chance to recover from the stress of the emergency.

Eager to take advantage of Dottie's suggestion, Alex made her way through the restaurant and out to the car as swiftly as she graciously could.

SHE WAS WORKING in her room that evening when Dottie tapped on the door. "Telephone, Alex."

"Thank you, Dottie. I'll take it in here." She lifted the receiver of the extension beside the bed. "Hello?"

"Everyone's been telling me I'm facing serious competition for my job."

"Don't you believe it," Alex answered, recognizing Kane's voice with a ripple of pleasure. "I never want to have to go through anything like that again."

Relax with **FOUR FREE** Romances plus two **FREE** gifts

Whatever the weather a Mills & Boon Romance provides an escape to relaxation and enjoyment. And as a special introductory offer we'll send you FOUR FREE Romances plus our cuddly teddy and a mystery gift when you complete and return this card. We'll also reserve you a subscription to our Reader Service which means you could go on to enjoy :

◆ **SIX BRAND NEW ROMANCES** sent direct to your door each month.

◆ **NO EXTRA CHARGES** free postage and packing.

◆ **OUR FREE MONTHLY NEWSLETTER** packed with competitions (with prizes such as televisions and free subscriptions), exclusive offers, horoscopes and much more.

◆ **HELPFUL FRIENDLY SERVICE** from our Customer Care team on 081-684-2141.

> Turn over to claim your FREE Romances, FREE cuddly teddy and mystery gift.

Plus a FREE cuddly teddy and special mystery gift.

Free Books and Gifts claim

Yes Please send me four Mills & Boon Romances, a cuddly teddy and mystery gift, absolutely FREE and without obligation. Please also reserve me a subscription to your Reader Service; which means that I can look forward to six brand new Romances for just £11.40 each month. Postage and packing are FREE along with all the benefits described overleaf. I understand that I may cancel or suspend my subscription at any time. However, if I decide not to subscribe I will write to you within 10 days. Any FREE books and gifts will remain mine to keep. I am over 18 years of age.

cuddly teddy   mystery gift

2A4R

Ms/Mrs/Miss/Mr _____

Address _____

_____

_____ Postcode _____

Signature _____

MAILING PREFERENCE SERVICE

Reader Service
FREEPOST
P.O. Box 236
Croydon
Surrey CR9 9EL

NO STAMP NEEDED

Send NO money now

"I'm sure you don't. But it's entirely probable that you and Tommy saved Zeb's life this afternoon. You did very well, Alex."

She'd had half a dozen calls of congratulations that afternoon, one from the editor of the small local newspaper, who wanted to feature her part in the rescue on the front page of the next issue, but Kane's praise meant more to her than any of the others. "Thank you, Kane. But I just did what anyone who'd studied CPR would have done. And Tommy was every bit as active as I was in administering it. I wouldn't have wanted to try to handle it on my own."

"But you could have," Kane murmured. "And would have tried."

She squirmed in self-conscious discomfort. "How is Zeb? Have you seen him?"

"Yes, I just left him in CICU. He's under a cardiologist's care and scheduled for open-heart surgery in the morning."

"Will he make it?"

"It's a little too early to predict at this point," Kane answered soberly. "But thanks to you and Tommy, he's got a fighting chance."

"You sound tired," Alex commented, turning the conversation away from herself.

"Yeah, I am. It's been a long day."

She found herself thinking wistfully of being with him, offering him a back rub, serving him a drink, or just sitting close to him as he rested. She blinked in startled disbelief at her unbidden fantasies. She'd certainly never pictured herself in that nurturing role with any other man! What had come over her lately? "Mmm . . . I suppose you'd better get some rest."

"Yeah, I think I will turn in. I'll see you in the morning, okay?"

"In the morning?"

"You have an appointment to have those stitches removed, remember?"

She groaned. "I'd forgotten," she admitted honestly. "It must be Freudian."

"Come on, Alex, it's not that bad. It won't hurt a bit."

"That's what all you doctors say," she muttered.

He chuckled. "I suppose you could always take them out yourself?"

"Oh, no. I'm giving up the medical profession. It's much too stressful."

"Then I'll see you at the clinic in the morning. I'm looking forward to getting my hands on you," he added, then hung up before Alex could decide whether he'd only been teasing.

She shivered at a sudden image of having Kane's hands on her—and not just on the stitches at her temple.

"DO YOU THINK Kane and Alex are still talking?" Dottie wondered aloud, glancing at the telephone in the living room.

"I'm sure he's simply complimenting her on her quick action in saving Zeb today," Mildred said, looking up from the book she'd been reading.

"Yes, she did handle that well, didn't she?"

Mildred closed the book with a snap. "You sound as though you take full credit!"

"I didn't say I had anything to do with it. It's only a coincidence that Zeb collapsed in that restaurant today, and you know very well I'd never wish that on anyone, but you have to admit that Alex handled the emergency beautifully."

"I've already said so, haven't I?"

"And are you beginning to understand why I think she is so right for Kane?"

"No," Mildred answered bluntly. "I don't. Just because she learned CPR in Chicago doesn't mean she fits into Kane's life here. It's not exactly something she'd be called upon to use on a regular basis. It's much more important that Kane finds someone who is involved with the normal, everyday routines of his life. Someone who can take care of him, not his patients. Someone like—"

"Melanie." Dottie and she finished in unison. "You're still determined to match them up, aren't you?"

"Being the mother of three children, Connie Travers is certainly good in a crisis," Johnnie Mae murmured with her usual vagueness. "One of those kids is always getting hurt, and she knows just what to do. She'd be a perfect doctor's wife."

"Some other doctor, perhaps. Kane seems quite taken with Alex," Dottie said emphatically.

"He's obviously quite fond of Melanie," Mildred declared flatly.

Johnnie Mae sighed and shook her head. "Frankly, I don't envy any of those young people right now."

6

ALEX WAS NOT looking forward to her visit to Kane's clinic Monday morning. Though she trusted his skill as a doctor, she still dreaded having the stitches removed, a process she feared would be painful. And then there was the situation between herself and Kane. But at least that shouldn't be a problem in such professional, rather public surroundings, she assured herself.

She'd learned from Dottie that Kane's partner was an older doctor on the verge of retirement, and that Kane was looking for a replacement. So many young doctors these days were looking for big-money, specialty positions in large cities, Dottie had added with a regretful sigh. The family practitioner was a rapidly disappearing breed. And Kane so desperately needed help with his caseload, especially since old Dr. Isaacs had cut back so sharply on his hours during the past year.

Despite Dottie's fussing about how busy Kane was, Alex was completely unprepared for the chaos that greeted her within the medical office. The waiting room was full of people who looked as though they'd been there awhile, two sick children were crying, an older man coughed noisily into a handkerchief. A crowd had gathered at the reception desk, where a tense-looking young woman in a nurse's uniform was scribbling what appeared to be a bill for a woman whose left arm was in a sling. A telephone rang repeatedly. Alex was just beginning to wonder if anyone was ever going to answer it, when Kane appeared from somewhere and snatched it up.

The doctor was answering the telephone? What in the world was going on here?

Kane spotted Alex as he hung up. He grimaced apologetically and stepped to one corner of the reception desk to greet her. "I'm running a little behind."

"So I see." She glanced again around the noisy, crowded waiting room. "Is it always like this?"

"It's *never* like this," he replied in obvious frustration. "Dr. Isaacs is out of town, and my front desk clerk is out with stomach flu."

"Dr. Lovell, will you be seeing me soon?" a man asked from the waiting area. "My appointment was for fifteen minutes ago."

"I'll be with you as soon as I can," Kane promised, then looked back at Alex. "The receptionist had to leave an hour after she arrived. My nurse and I have been trying to handle everything, but it's getting away from us."

"Why in the world didn't you call for assistance? Doesn't Andersenville have a temp agency?"

"Dr. Lovell, Dr. Westfield is on line one," the nurse called out. "What should I tell him?"

"Tell him I'll call back, will you, Tina?" He turned back to Alex. "No, we don't have a temp agency. I tried calling Mother, but she's at one of her meetings. Frankly, I just don't know...."

"Take care of your patients, Kane," Alex ordered, shrugging out of her jacket. "I'll take over here."

"You? But—"

"Dr. Lovell?" a timid voice asked from behind Alex. "Timmy's fever seems to be going up."

"Go take care of your patients, Kane," Alex repeated, rounding the desk. "Your nurse can give me quick instructions here, and then she'll be back to help you."

Kane sighed and ran a hand through his hair. "I don't know how I'll ever thank you for this."

"Don't try. I'll consider it research," she said with a smile.

"Okay, Mrs. Rogers, bring Timmy on back to the examining room," Kane instructed, already looking less harried.

"I'm Alex Bennett," Alex said to the nurse. "Tell me what to do out here and you can get back to your work."

"I wish I knew what to tell you," Tina answered apologetically, pushing a loose strand of brown hair out of her eyes. "I never worked the desk before. I've only worked for Dr. Lovell for a couple of months. I've just been writing down the names of the people who come in, trying to find their files and making out these bills from the payment schedule the doctor fills out after each examination. Oh, and answering the phone. Here's the appointment book. There's a little note clipped to the front that gives an approximate exam time for different reasons—like physicals, or prenatal checks, that sort of thing."

Alex stared at the piles of papers on the desk in disbelief. "But where's the computer?"

"We don't have a computer. Everything's still done by hand or typewriter," Tina admitted.

No computer? Alex hadn't thought there were any offices, no matter how small and rural, that hadn't yet entered the high-tech age!

"Excuse me," a hoarse voice said from the other side of the desk, "but I have an appointment with Dr. Lovell."

"Tina!" Kane's voice called from down a hallway. "Can you give me a hand here?"

Tina gave Alex an apologetic look of sympathy. "Good luck," she said, and turned to hurry away.

"Do you think the doctor's going to be much longer? I've got to get back to work," the same impatient man from earlier complained.

"Ma'am? I have an eleven o'clock appointment with the doctor. Is he running behind?"

"Excuse me, but where are the rest rooms?"

The telephone rang again. Alex gulped and made an effort to split her attention four ways. It was going to be a very long day, she decided. But at least she had an excellent excuse to delay having her stitches out for a few hours longer!

NEITHER ALEX, KANE nor Tina had a chance to eat lunch that day. Thanks to a couple of last-minute cancellations, including the appointment Alex had made for that morning, Kane was able to make up lost time after she took over the desk, though he ran a few minutes behind for the rest of the day.

They worked out a system, of sorts, Alex asking Tina
or Kane for assistance only when necessary, Kane letting her know through coded notes which patients
could be billed later and the ones he wanted to pay on
their way out. Alex made detailed notes for the regular
clerical staff, clipping them neatly to the patient files,
hoping she hadn't made any irreversible mistakes. She
made no effort to deal with insurance companies. That,
she decided, was for someone who knew what she was
doing. Any insurance questions were recorded on more
notes and clipped to the corresponding folders.

The telephone rang constantly. She took messages
when necessary, asked callers who were requesting
nonemergency appointments to please call back the
next day—she certainly hoped this was a short-lived flu
epidemic!—and passed calls she couldn't handle to
Kane or Tina. She didn't know how she was doing it,
exactly, but somehow she managed to bring a sem-
blance of order to the pandemonium that had greeted
her earlier.

"I've never seen a more antiquated filing system in my
entire life," she couldn't help muttering to Kane at one
breathing point during the afternoon. "Why in the
world haven't you gotten computers for your poor
staff?"

"I haven't had time to deal with it," he admitted. "Dr.
Isaacs never caught up with the computer age, and most
of my staff tend to be computerphobic. I have a PC of
my own, of course, but I haven't gotten around to
training them to use it. I've had quite a few salespeople
calling on me lately, trying to sell me software and sup-

port for medical clinics. I just haven't had a chance to sit down and look over their materials."

"It would certainly make your billing and record keeping easier," Alex told him, well aware that she was treading in an area that wasn't exactly her business. "I minored in computer sciences in college, so I know a bit about the software available for businesses like this one," she explained. "Your staff would be amazed at how simple they can be to operate, once they get past the initial wariness."

Kane lifted an eyebrow. "Maybe you'd have time to look over some of the brochures I've been given?" he suggested diffidently. "I've been meaning to ask Melanie to take a glance at them—I understand she's quite computer-literate—but . . ."

"I'd be happy to look them over," Alex heard herself volunteering quickly, though she couldn't for the life of her imagine why she suddenly seemed so compelled to do so. "Er . . . not that I'm an expert on the subject or anything," she added less confidently.

"I'd appreciate your suggestions," Kane assured her with a smile.

"Dr. Lovell?"

Kane's smile turned to a wry grimace, he signaled to his nurse that he'd be right with her. "Duty calls."

Alex was already reaching for the telephone, which had begun to ring again.

THE LAST PATIENT finally left, the office day ended and Alex was able to switch on the answering machine and lock the front door. "Whew!" she said, turning wearily to Kane. "Whatever you're paying your office staff, it isn't enough."

"You're right," he agreed. "Starting tomorrow, they all get raises. Now, about your stitches . . ."

She'd forgotten all about them again. She cleared her throat. "We could always wait another day."

"No, we won't wait another day. We're both here, we've got some free time, and there's no reason to put it off any longer. So," he said, stepping closer and lowering his voice a half octave. "Go on into exam room two and take off your clothes. I'll be with you shortly," he added in a mock-serious tone of voice.

"Nice try, Doc, but I'm not about to take off my clothes to have stitches removed from my temple," Alex replied dryly.

He grinned. "Well, hell. You take all the fun out of playing doctor."

"Watch it, or you'll find yourself slapped with a malpractice suit," she warned, trying unsuccessfully to keep from smiling back at him. He really did have the nicest smile, she thought wistfully.

Stepping into the room he'd indicated, she looked a bit nervously at the paper-covered examination table, trying not to think about the stitch-removal process. She entertained herself, instead, with giddy fantasies about stripping off her clothes and giving Kane's hands something else to occupy them. Then she chided herself for allowing his casual little joke to send her unusually active hormones into overdrive. She actually blushed a bit when Kane walked into the room, though she tried to hide the reaction by turning away from him as she climbed onto the edge of the table.

For the first time during that crazy, busy day, she noted how devastatingly attractive he looked in the white coat he wore with a blue shirt, striped tie and dark blue dress slacks. All the commotion earlier had defused some of the tension between them. Now it was just the two of them again, and Alex found herself more aware of him than ever. She swallowed hard, determined to be professional about this. She was the patient, he was the doctor, and that was all there was to it.

Yeah, right, Alexandra. And if you believe that, someone should sell you some swampland in Florida.

She groaned.

He grinned, obviously misinterpreting it. "You're not afraid, are you? I promise I'll be gentle."

"That's what you keep telling me."

"Trust me, Alex."

She swallowed hard at his almost intimate tone. "Mmm . . . don't you need Tina to help you?" she asked when he picked up a tiny pair of scissors from a tray on a nearby credenza.

His smile deepened the dimples at either side of his mouth. "This is hardly major surgery. Tina just left. I guess I could try to flag her down if you're that uncomfortable. . . ."

"No, of course not," Alex muttered, squirming self-consciously against the crinkly white paper beneath her bottom. "I was just wondering."

As he'd promised, Kane was gentle with the removal of her stitches, though it was still an uncomfortable process, as far as Alex was concerned. She was relieved when he announced that he'd taken out the last one.

"You can let go of my coat now," he added, his voice holding just a hint of laughter.

Startled, she looked down, to find herself holding the hem of his coat in a white-knuckled grip. She let go immediately, feeling her face warming. "Sorry."

"No problem. Are you this nervous with every doctor, or is it just with me?"

"With every doctor," she admitted. "I try to avoid all members of the medical profession whenever possible."

He frowned, still standing close to her. "I hope that doesn't mean you avoid regular medical checkups," he scolded mildly. "You should have a pelvic examination and a pap smear every year, as well as . . ."

Her face burning in earnest now, Alex interrupted him hastily. "Of course I have regular checkups, Kane. I'm not that careless with my health."

And she had absolutely no intention of saying any more on *that* subject, she added mentally. No way was she going to sit here, discussing pelvic exams and pap smears and whatever with Kane Lovell, even if he was a doctor!

He nodded in apparent satisfaction. "Good. Your health is far too important to take for granted."

"So, are you finished with my head?" she asked, nearly cringing at the strained, rather high-pitched sound of her voice.

He chuckled at her wording and nodded. "All done," he assured her. She became speechless when he framed her face between his skillful hands. "I haven't really thanked you for what you did for me today, have I?"

She cleared her throat forcefully, intensely aware that her knees were pressed against his thigh as he stood close to the end of the table on which she sat. All she had to do was shift them another inch or so ... She forced her attention to the conversation. "It really isn't necessary, Kane. I'm glad I was able to help out, especially after all you've done for me."

"I still want to thank you," he murmured. "My way."

Then he kissed her, and Alex closed her eyes and melted into him, as though she'd been waiting for this all day.

The kiss was long and deep, a thorough, mutual exploration of tastes and textures. When it ended, Alex's arms were around Kane's neck, and he was no longer standing against her knees but between them. So closely between them that she was well aware how deeply he'd been affected by the embrace. Not that she could have disguised her own reaction: pounding pulse, ragged breathing and heavy eyelids. Dammit, he'd made her tingle again! All over her body, this time.

She stared at him, waiting for him to say something, trying to think of something to say to him.

Kane cleared his throat, though his voice was still husky when he spoke. "Let me know if that cut gives you any more trouble," he said, stepping back quickly. "I'll bring those brochures over for you to look at, whenever I get a chance."

Cut? Brochures? Who could think of anything so mundane after a kiss like that? Had she been the only one to find it the most extraordinary experience of her life?

"I'd better get on over to the hospital for my evening rounds," Kane went on as though he hadn't noticed that she was still temporarily incapable of speech. He avoided her eyes and gathered the instruments he'd used to remove her stitches. "I'm sure you're ready to get home and unwind. You certainly didn't expect your appointment to include a full day's work, did you?"

Alex slid silently off the table.

"D'you need any help getting out to your car? I have a few more things to do here yet."

She shook her head and forced herself to speak, relieved that her voice came out relatively normally. "I'll be fine. Mmm . . . you'll have me billed for the—?"

"Don't be absurd," he interrupted brusquely. "I should be paying you for everything you did for me today."

"Let's just call it even," she murmured, turning toward the door.

"Alex?" he said, when she was halfway into the hallway.

She paused and looked over her shoulder, to find him watching her with an expression she couldn't begin to read. "Yes?"

He pushed his hands into the pockets of his lab coat. "I'll talk to you later."

She sensed that he'd started to say something else but had changed his mind. She nodded and turned away, her head still spinning from Kane's very intoxicating bedside manner.

KANE CALLED HIMSELF an idiot, even as he gathered the software brochures and headed for the back door of his house that evening. It was getting late, and he'd had no intention of seeing Alex again that day, but something was drawing him over there. He knew he was being a fool to spend more time with her. He knew, as well, that he'd never get to sleep if he didn't give in to this overwhelming urge.

Seeing someone moving around behind the kitchen curtains, he tapped on the door, hoping he wouldn't disturb any members of the household who might already be in bed. His mother flicked back the curtain on the door, then opened it quickly. "Kane? What is it?"

He held up the stack of brochures. "Alex offered to look over some computer information for me. Is she still up?"

"Yes, I think so," Dottie answered, eyeing him with obvious speculation. "Though she looked tired when she came home. She told us what happened. You must have been so grateful to her for helping out today."

"I was. Very grateful."

"Is she expecting you tonight?"

"No," Kane admitted. "I just wanted to see her—er, I mean, give her these things. Here," he said abruptly, holding out the brochures. "you can just give them to her later. There's no need to bother her tonight."

Dottie backed away quickly, making no effort to take the pamphlets from him. "I'm sure Alex won't mind. I'll go get her."

She was gone before Kane could call her back. He sighed and leaned against a counter to wait for Alex, wishing he'd just stayed at home.

ALEX'S HEART WAS BEATING rapidly in her throat when she entered the kitchen, finding Kane waiting for her with shuttered eyes and an enigmatic smile. "Mmm...your mother said to tell you good-night. She's turning in. Johnnie Mae and Mildred are already in bed for the night."

He nodded. "I hope I'm not disturbing you."

"No, of course not. I was just working on my notes. I don't usually go to bed quite this early." She hadn't really been working, of course. She'd been staring for hours at a blank sheet of paper, mentally reliving their kiss, trying to convince herself it had only been an expression of gratitude on Kane's part. That it hadn't really changed her entire life, though she'd had the oddest feeling that the kiss had permanently affected her in some way she couldn't yet define. "What was it you wanted, Kane?"

He nodded toward the stack of pamphlets and brochures he'd set on the table. "I brought that software information I told you about this morning. I was hoping you'd find time to look it over and make some recommendations for me."

Alex glanced at the stack, then turned back to Kane. "I'd be happy to look at it," she said, then added candidly, "but I warn you, Kane, I'm no expert on medical office software. You'll probably need to talk in depth to some of the salespeople."

He nodded again. "I know, and I will when I get a chance. But you know computers better than I do. You may have a suggestion that will save me some time."

"I'll try," she repeated, shoving her hands into the pockets of the jeans she'd worn to his office that morning along with the bright red sweater she still had on. She was suddenly unsure what to say next. Had he really come over only to give her these materials? If so, why hadn't he just left them with Dottie?

Kane shoved himself away from the counter, abruptly standing upright. He ran a hand through his hair. "I guess that's all, then. Uh . . . any more problems with your head? Any tenderness?"

She resisted an impulse to lift a hand to the faint, slightly reddened scar at her temple, afraid he'd see that her hand wasn't entirely steady if she took it out of her pocket. "It's fine. Thank you."

"Good. Well . . . you'd probably like to get back to work. Thanks for looking this stuff over for me, Alex."

"You're welcome," she replied, oddly disappointed that she could think of no reason to detain him any longer.

He hesitated a moment more, then turned toward the door. He had a hand on the doorknob when he looked back over his shoulder. "You know," he said with an uncharacteristic hint of uncertainty, "it's really a beautiful evening. Would you like to sit on the lawn swing with me for a little while? Talk a little, have a soda or something, maybe?"

Did he plan to talk about the kiss they'd shared? Was he expecting to repeat it? "I'd like that," Alex heard herself agreeing without even taking a moment to think about it. "I bought some soft drinks this afternoon. Want one?"

He nodded and opened the door. "Sounds good. Meet you at the lawn swing."

She took a moment after he stepped outside to wonder what in the world she was doing. Then she pushed the question to the back of her mind, ran a smoothing hand over her dark curls, and grabbed two cans out of the refrigerator. She and Kane were only going to talk, she reminded herself, letting herself out the door. Nothing at all to worry about, right?

He hadn't exaggerated about the evening. It *was* beautiful. Just cool enough to be refreshing. The sky clear and star-filled. A full moon. Frogs and crickets doing their nightly thing, filling the crisp, fragrant air with sound. Off in the distance, a dog barked. And was that . . . ?

She frowned a bit and sat down on the freestanding, redwood lawn swing beside Kane, handing him a drink as she spoke. "Do you hear a cow mooing?"

Kane laughed softly and popped the tab on the can. "What is this cow obsession of yours?"

She smiled self-consciously and shook her head, carefully opening her own drink. "Never mind. Probably just my imagination."

Kane set the swing into gentle motion with one foot. Alex tried to look relaxed and comfortable, though she felt anything but. Usually able to make casual conversation even with strangers, she suddenly found herself incapable of thinking of a word to say. Maybe it was because sitting so very close to Kane on such a quiet, beautiful evening was making her mouth go dry. She sipped her cola.

"How long have you been writing, Alex?" Kane asked, obviously trying to fill the silence between them.

"Almost as long as I can remember," she replied, smiling faintly as she thought of long, solitary hours in her childhood bedroom, her only companions a record player and a stack of wire-bound notebooks. "But my first book was published four years ago," she added more specifically. "I've had three published since that one."

"You've done quite well in your career to have been at it such a short time."

"Thank you. I've been pleased with the success I've had." That, of course, was a major understatement. Alex wasn't sure what she'd have done if she hadn't found success with her writing. There had never been anything else she'd wanted that badly, any other dream that had driven her, any other passion as all consuming.

"What about you, Kane?" she asked, turning the questioning back on him. "Have you always wanted to be a doctor?"

He smiled. "Since I broke my leg, riding my bike, when I was nine. I was intrigued by the whole process, when Dr. Isaacs set the leg and made it whole and straight again. Then I had my tonsils out and that just iced the cake."

Alex giggled. "You *enjoyed* having your tonsils out?"

He grinned sheepishly. "Well, yeah. I mean, I didn't like the discomfort—I'm no masochist—but the hospital procedures fascinated me. The whole idea of healing, battling illnesses and injuries and saving lives . . ."

He stopped and shook his head; his tone became self-deprecating. "One of my college roommates called it a divinity complex. I don't know. Maybe he was right. There's a certain thrill of power in taking on a deadly illness and coming out the victor."

"I'm sure there is," Alex agreed softly. "But that isn't really why you do it, is it, Kane? If you were only in it for the power or the wealth, you wouldn't have set up practice in rural Mississippi, where most of your patients have little extra money to spend on fancy medical procedures. The truth is, you love helping people. Easing their pain. Delivering their babies. Saving their lives when you get the chance."

He squirmed self-consciously on the wooden seat of the swing. "I thought you said all doctors were arrogant and proprietary toward their patients—or, as you called them, subjects."

She nodded. "Yes, sometimes that, too."

"Does that mean you can't quite make up your mind about me?"

"Oh, I think you're a nice enough guy," she said, trying to speak lightly. "A true humanitarian. But I also think you'd be a very difficult man to become . . . well, involved with."

His brows lifted. "And why is that?"

She rather wished she'd never started this. But, since she had, she felt compelled to answer frankly. "A woman involved with you would have to be prepared to share you. With your work, your patients, your family. She'd have to expect to have dinners interrupted, vacations canceled, family functions missed. She'd have to accept being in second place and be content with whatever you had left to give her. Loving a workaholic can be a very painful exercise in self-sacrifice."

Kane winced. "Seems like I've heard this lecture before," he murmured.

A hint of bitterness in his voice made Alex look at him searchingly. "Someone who couldn't take second place?" she asked quietly.

"Someone who wouldn't even give it a chance," he returned with a slight shrug. "Someone who'd thought she could convince me to get into dermatology or podiatry or some other generally emergency-free specialty, and then to take a cushy, overpaid position in a fancy hospital in some big, bustling city. When she finally realized that I was determined to come back to Nowhere, Mississippi, as she called it, and to set up a family practice, she found someone whose goals were more like her own."

"She hurt you." It wasn't a question. Alex could still hear the old pain behind his clipped words.

"She broke my heart." He pressed a hand to his chest and spoke in an overly dramatic, mocking voice, clearly meant to hide the truth behind the words. It didn't quite work.

Alex touched his arm. "I'm sorry."

He shrugged, not looking at her. "It was a long time ago. I was just finishing med school. I got over her."

But he hadn't gotten over the disappointment, Alex realized. She guessed that Kane would have been very careful in his relationships since, making sure there was no question of his dedication to his work, keeping women at a slight distance until he judged their compatibility with his life-style. He'd kissed her until her ears had buzzed . . . but she was probably much different from the women Kane usually dated. She imagined that Melanie would be much more the type of a mate he would look for.

This time it was Kane who redirected the questioning. "You sound as though you've had some experience of being involved with a workaholic. The boyfriend in Chicago?"

"Hardly," Alex replied lightly. "Both my parents were workaholics. Serious ones. I was always amazed that they remembered my birthday every year. Bill's just the opposite. He likes his job—he's a commercial loan officer—but when working hours are done, he leaves his work in the office. He'd rather spend his off hours having dinner out, attending the theater or the symphony or playing tennis. He's quite good at tennis, actually. He even thought of going pro when he was in college."

"Well, isn't that interesting." Kane smiled grimly to counter the rather vicious edge he heard in his voice. "He forecloses on struggling small businessmen during the day, then relaxes with a brisk game of tennis or an evening at the symphony."

Alex bit her lip against a smile. "He's hardly a business shark. Bill's almost too softhearted for his own good, when it comes to struggling small businessmen. He's been known to lend them money out of his own pocket, when he knows the bank won't look twice at them. And he's rarely lost money doing so. They almost always pay him back. He's a nice guy."

"Oh." Kane rocked the swing a bit more forcefully before speaking again, his gaze apparently focused on his house next door. "So, are you and he . . . er . . . ?"

"He's asked me to marry him," Alex answered softly. She wasn't quite sure why she was telling him. Maybe just to see what he'd say in response.

Whatever reaction Kane might have had to her words wasn't apparent in his expression or his voice. Neither changed in the slightest. "And you said . . . ?"

"That I needed time to think about it."

He gave her a sideways glance, one eyebrow lifted. "He sounds like a great catch. What's holding you back?"

"Maybe I'm not looking for a great catch," she answered cuttingly.

"What *are* you looking for?"

She shrugged. "Maybe I'm not looking at all."

He set his drink upon the small, wrought iron table in front of the swing and half turned to face her. "Everyone's looking, Alex. But not everyone's lucky enough to know what they want—or to find it if they do know."

"What about you, Kane?" she asked, her own drink clutched in suddenly nerveless fingers. "Do you know what you're looking for?"

"I thought I did," he murmured, lifting a hand to toy with a curl at her cheek. "Now I'm not so sure."

Her mouth went dry. "Kane . . ."

He slipped the can from her hand and set it beside his own. "I want to kiss you, Alex. Are you going to punch me if I do?"

She couldn't smile at his deliberately whimsical tone, though she knew he was giving her an out if she wanted it. "No," she whispered, her hand going up to his chest as he leaned toward her. "But I'm not sure this is wise, Kane."

"Probably not wise at all," he agreed huskily. "But that doesn't stop me from wanting it. Wanting you," he added, sliding his fingers into her hair. "Alex . . ."

She'd never know which of them closed the distance between them. But suddenly her arms were around his neck, his hands flattened against her back, and their mouths were locked together in exactly the type of kiss she'd wanted from him, almost from the first moment she'd seen him. Deep. Hot. Hungry.

She'd thought he'd be gentle. He wasn't.

She'd have guessed there'd be some uncertainty, some tentativeness in their first real kiss. There wasn't.

She'd hoped she'd be able to kiss him without losing herself in him. She couldn't.

His hands swept her back, pressing her closer, exploring her slender curves through her soft sweater. She tangled her fingers in his hair, holding his mouth more tightly to her own. He pulled back at last for a gasp of air, but then he was kissing her again, just as deeply, just as desperately.

She shivered when he slipped one hand between them to cup one of her breasts. Again, she'd expected his touch to be more hesitant, giving her every chance to stop him if this wasn't what she wanted. But even as his strong, clever fingers closed over her, she knew she wouldn't have stopped him, if he had given her a choice. This was exactly what she wanted. And Kane knew it as well as she did.

She could feel the heat of him through his shirt. Could feel the muscles bunch beneath her palms when she slid her hands slowly down his back. She ached to feel his warm skin pressed to hers. Her hand fell to his rock-hard thigh as he slid his thumb slowly, firmly over one swollen nipple. She gasped into his mouth in immediate reaction.

Kane tore his mouth from hers. "Alex," he muttered roughly, clenching his free hand into the hair at the back of her head to turn her face up to his. "I want you."

She moved her hand an inch inward, brushing the obvious hardness beneath his close-fitting slacks. "I know," she whispered.

He shuddered at her touch, his fingers tightening almost painfully in her hair. He loosened them immediately. "Come home with me, Alex. Now. Please."

She wanted to agree so badly that she trembled with the need to do so. But her tremors were also caused by fear. Making love with Kane wouldn't be casual. It wouldn't be insignificant. And it wouldn't be something she'd forget. Maybe ever.

She'd always been careful. Always in control. But she couldn't stay in control of these feelings for Kane, couldn't keep them tidy and manageable. She wanted him as she'd never wanted anyone before. And the depth of that wanting terrified her.

"Kane . . ."

He kissed her quickly, as though sensing she was going to refuse. As though hoping he was wrong.

"Don't say no, Alex," he whispered, his lips moving persuasively against hers. "I want you. It would be good between us."

She could feel herself weakening, even as his lips settled again over hers. He shifted on the rocking swing until his thigh pressed more firmly against her, making her achingly aware of the extent of his arousal. Her own desire flared in response. She parted her lips, welcomed his tongue with her own, she flattened her breasts against his chest.

"Alex." His voice was raw, gritty. "Come home with me."

"I . . ."

Later, she'd wonder what she would have said. She'd suspect it might have been yes. But whatever it might have been was cut off by a shrill, annoying, repetitive beeping that sliced through the silence surrounding them.

It took her desire-dazed mind a moment to identify the sound. When Kane cursed beneath his breath, she glanced downward in comprehension. He pressed a button on the small, plastic box clipped to his belt, and the beeping stopped.

"I have to go," he groaned, his fist clenching on his thigh. "Alex, I'm sorry."

She took a deep breath, struggling to regain her composure. Her hair had tumbled around her face. She pushed it back with unsteady hands. "I understand."

He sighed and tucked one stray curl behind her ear, his touch suddenly gentle. "Are you okay?"

"Yes, of course. You'd better go. At this hour, it's probably an emergency."

"More likely Darla Kingrey's baby," he said ruefully; he pushed himself reluctantly off the swing. "It's due any day."

"Then I hope it's a safe delivery—and a healthy baby," she said more lightly than she felt, not quite meeting his eyes. "Good night, Kane."

"Alex, I—" He stopped, uttered another curse, then shook his head. "I'm sorry," he repeated. "But you were right earlier. This is my life."

"I know," she managed to say through a tight smile.

He shoved a hand through his disheveled hair, glancing toward his mother's house, obviously anxious to respond to the call. "I'll see you in."

"No. I think I'll sit out here awhile, finish my drink."

He nodded. "Good night, Alex. I'll talk to you tomorrow." She couldn't bring herself to reply.

A moment later Kane was gone and she was alone in the shadows, the only sounds the dull roar of his car engine, fading down the street, and the insects that sang on, oblivious to the human drama going on around them. Soothing her tight, hot throat with a long swallow of her cola, she concentrated fiercely on those sounds, refusing to think about Kane, about what might have been between them.

7

ALEX FOUND HERSELF joining the others dining at Melanie Chastain's house on Thursday evening. Her housemates had swept her along with them, insisting that Melanie would be terribly disappointed if Alex didn't go. Melanie, Mildred added sweetly, was *such* a good cook.

And she was, of course, Alex discovered during the four-course, gourmet meal their hostess had obviously worked hours to prepare. Everything was perfect.

Melanie had probably never made any of the mistakes Alex had managed during her few, disastrous attempts at cooking for guests. Like accidentally substituting salt for sugar. Or using baking soda instead of baking powder. Or mistaking chili powder for paprika—or forgetting to cover a chicken and rice casserole before baking it, resulting in a hard, dry mess in the bottom of a dish.

It wasn't that Alex was incapable of reading labels or following recipes. It was just that she usually had more important things on her mind, she'd tried to rationalize on occasion. Everyone had her own talents—Alex was a writer, not a cook.

Unfortunately, Melanie Chastain appeared to have many talents. She could probably sit down and whip out a Pulitzer-prizewinning novel if she set her mind to it, Alex thought with a silent sigh.

"Melanie, this is delicious," Kane raved during the main course. "You cook almost as well as my mother," he added with a wink for Dottie.

"Nice save," Dottie murmured, smiling at him.

Melanie blushed charmingly at Kane's praise. "Why, thank you. I enjoy cooking."

Alex hadn't seen Kane since the interlude on the lawn swing Monday evening. She'd gone out of her way to avoid him for the first day or two after that, until she realized that it wasn't necessary. He'd made no effort to track her down.

She'd wondered if he regretted the words spoken in the heat of passion. For her part, she'd spent many hours trying to convince herself that it had been for the best that Kane had been called away before their caresses had gone any further.

"It's such a shame more young women these days aren't interested in learning traditional homemaking skills," Mildred stated emphatically, breaking into Alex's thoughts. "Every woman should know how to cook."

Mildred didn't look at Alex as she spoke. But then, she didn't really have to, Alex reflected.

"Modern technology has made it possible for every woman—and every man, for that matter—to prepare a nutritious, good-tasting meal without spending hours in the kitchen," Dottie replied, sounding oddly defensive. On Alex's behalf, perhaps? "Microwaves and frozen entrées are probably the greatest inventions ever for working parents."

"Frozen entrées," Mildred said in disgust. "As though you'd have ever served anything like that to Kane."

"I would have, occasionally, if they'd been as good as they are now," Dottie retorted. "Or if I'd worked full-time out of the home," she added.

Alex cleared her throat. "I can hardly boil water, but I order takeout a lot in Chicago. I manage to eat well without cooking much."

Johnnie Mae giggled. "The only delivery places around here serve pizza. That's okay for most folks, but I'm allergic to tomato sauce. I break out in huge splotches every time I get near it."

"Alex, I understand you spoke to Emily's tenth-graders today," Kane said, smoothly changing the subject.

It was the first time he'd spoken directly to her all evening, but Alex was so grateful he'd distracted the others from their discussion of domestic skills. "Yes, I did. I had a great time with them. They asked some interesting questions."

Kane chuckled. "I'm sure they did."

"You like children, Alex?" Dottie asked, smiling at her across the table.

"I haven't been around small children much, but I enjoy the older ones when I speak to them. They're always so energetic and creative."

"Melanie loves children. Even small ones," Mildred announced. "Don't you, dear?"

Looking a bit embarrassed that Mildred kept singling her out that way, Melanie nodded. "Yes, I'm very fond of children."

"Melanie was baby-sitting by the time she was twelve," Pearl added, joining in the singing of her granddaughter's praises. "She didn't even ask to be paid, half the time. And you should see her with her little niece and nephew. They adore their Aunt Melanie."

Alex concentrated on finishing her dinner, wondering why she was suddenly feeling like the runner-up in a two-woman contest. And then she glanced up from her food to find Kane's eyes on her. In their depths she could almost see the memory of their heated kisses on a romantically shadowed lawn swing. As her gaze locked with his, she moistened her lips, as if she could still taste him there. The heat in his eyes suddenly intensified—was she just imagining it?

Acutely aware of the others, Alex glanced down the table toward Melanie. She found the young woman watching her—and Kane—with a thoughtful expression that made her uncomfortable.

Maybe it was time to start thinking of going back to Chicago, she thought bleakly. As much as she was enjoying Andersenville and its warm, eccentric residents, she could only foresee painful complications if she allowed herself to become more deeply involved in the lives of these people. She was the outsider at this table, the one who didn't really belong.

If only she had something to look forward to. Chicago and its routine seemed increasingly monotonous. And then there was Bill, who'd be expecting an answer to his proposal when she returned. She knew she couldn't accept that proposal, yet she dreaded talking to him again. She didn't want to hurt him, she didn't want a scene. But mostly, she regretted having to admit that she'd failed at yet another relationship.

Maybe she was destined to live the rest of her life alone with her work and her few hobbies. Maybe she should buy a cat.

"Alex? Is something wrong?" Dottie asked quietly, in a slightly concerned tone.

Realizing her pensive mood must be written all over her face, Alex forced a smile and shook her head. "No, of course not. I was just . . . er . . . wondering about Melanie's work. Tell me more about the retail business, Melanie. Do you handle the buying for your store yourself?"

"Most of it," Melanie replied graciously. "It's not a very big store—mostly practical, moderately-priced family clothing. But we also carry lingerie, accessories and a few gift and cosmetic items. I'd like to expand the gift department. Perhaps add a slightly more expensive line of professional women's clothing. With Andersenville growing, the way it has been in the past few years, I see the need for slightly more sophisticated merchandise, the kind my father stocked when he opened the store twenty years ago."

The future and progress of the area became the main topic of conversation for the remainder of the evening in Melanie's small, tastefully furnished house. Alex had learned that Melanie had moved into the gracefully aging, frame home next door to her grandmother for much the same reasons Kane had chosen to build next to his mother. Obviously both of them believed it was their responsibility to take care of the older members of their respective families.

Kane had a great deal in common with Melanie, actually. Much more than he did with her, Alex thought as the evening drew to a congenial end.

Kane was the first to leave, explaining that he had early rounds the next morning. He thanked Melanie warmly for the dinner, praised her culinary talents one last time, then took his leave of the others without lingering. He didn't quite meet Alex's eyes as he bade her good-night, nor did she try to detain him, though she was still tingling from that exchange of glances over the dinner table.

Pearl drew Dottie, Mildred and Johnnie Mae outside for a few minutes to admire the small brick patio Melanie had recently commissioned beyond the sliding glass doors in her tiny living room. Alex found herself for the first time alone with Melanie when she insisted on helping her tidy the kitchen, which was barely large enough to hold the two of them.

"You've made a very nice home for yourself here," Alex commented, admiring the assortment of fresh herbs growing in a window box over the sink.

Melanie smiled and wiped a damp cloth over the already spotless, yellow countertop. "Thanks. It's small, but it's really all the space I need. And I like living close to my grandmother, so I can keep an eye on her. Her health isn't as good as it used to be, but she doesn't want to move out of her own place yet. This way we both have some privacy, yet I can discreetly watch out for her."

"Very clever."

"Well, it's working for now, anyway. Since my father died and my mother moved in with my sister in

Georgia, my grandmother's the only family I have here. We're very close."

"You didn't mind moving back here after college, then?"

"No. I always knew I wanted to take over the store someday. That's what I trained to do, what I planned from the time I was very young. I only wish my father could have lived longer," Melanie added sadly. "I didn't want to take over under these circumstances. I had expected to work and study for a few more years in the larger retail market in Saint Louis, which is where I was when Dad had his heart attack."

"I'm very sorry about your father," Alex murmured, hearing the lingering grief in the other woman's voice.

"Thank you. It helped that I had a lot of close friends here. They were wonderful to my family and me."

"One of the advantages to life in a small town, I suppose."

"One of many, as far as I'm concerned." Melanie smiled. "But I'm hardly objective, since I was born and raised here. Quite happily, for the most part."

"Kane seems to feel the same way," Alex commented lightly, keeping her gaze focused on one of the delicate plants on the windowsill.

"Yes, I suppose he does, since he could have practiced anywhere he wanted. My grandmother said he was offered several, very impressive positions in big cities, when he finished his residency, but he chose to come back here, instead. He ... was engaged at the time," she added rather hesitantly. "His fiancée was furious at his choice. She'd wanted him to take one of those other jobs, even though he'd told her from the beginning that he wanted to live here. Maybe she thought she could change his mind."

Her back still turned to Melanie, Alex lifted an eyebrow. Melanie, the perfect young lady, was actually gossiping? How uncharacteristic. Was there a reason behind the slip? Was Melanie subtly testing Alex's feelings for Kane? Trying to learn if Alex was another big-city resident who had no interest in small-town, Southern living?

Since she hadn't allowed herself to analyze her feelings for Kane, or to speculate on a possible future for them beyond the major obstacle of his total dedication to his work, Alex wasn't sure what to say to Melanie. Actually, she would have liked to do a little digging herself. Just how serious was Melanie about Kane?

Instead, Alex chose to respond rather vaguely to Melanie's comment. "It's always a mistake to become involved with someone while hoping to change them."

"Yes." Melanie wiped the countertop a bit harder. "Kane's a nice man, isn't he?"

Alex stared more intently at the herbs. "Yes, very. I suppose you've known him all your life?"

"Oh, no. He's several years older than I am, so I didn't know him in school. Actually, we've only known each other for a few weeks."

"Oh."

"I think . . ." Melanie cleared her throat delicately. "I think Mildred and my grandmother are trying to play matchmaker for Kane and me. It's becoming embarrassing."

Alex looked over her shoulder then, noting Melanie's heightened color. "You're ... er ... not interested?"

Melanie shrugged rather helplessly. "How can I tell? I've hardly spoken two words to him in private. He seems nice, as I said, but... Well, that's about it, so far, you know? I mean, I'd probably go out with him if he asked, just to get to know him better, but he hasn't asked."

"I understand his job keeps him very busy." Alex offered the excuse rather weakly.

"Yes. That doesn't really bother me, since I have a demanding job of my own. But somehow I don't think his work is all that's holding Kane back." Melanie took a quick breath, then said "I think it's you Kane would like to ask out."

"Look, Melanie, I—"

"Really, Alex. I've seen the sparks between the two of you. I mean, they'd be hard to miss. "

"But I—"

Melanie smiled and suddenly patted Alex's arm. "I'm sorry. I'm embarrassing you. I just wanted you to know that it wouldn't bother me if you go out with him. It's not as though I have any claim to him, or even want one, at this point. I'm really not in a hurry to get seriously involved with any man. But what I *would* like is a friend. There aren't that many single women in town. Most of the ones my age have married or moved away. And I want to be your friend, at least, while you're in town. I'd like for us to be able to see a movie or go shopping together or something, without any awkwardness over my grandmother's scheming."

Alex was touched by the sincerity in Melanie's voice. She hadn't realized that Melanie had been lonely since moving back to town, her time divided primarily between taking on a new job and taking care of her grandmother. Though Alex couldn't guarantee that she'd be in Andersenville much longer, she, too, would like to know she had a friend while she was there. And she'd liked Melanie Chastain from the first, despite her exasperation with Melanie's daunting attributes.

"I'd like that, too, Melanie. I've spent so many evenings with my notes and my computer that I'm starting to feel like a recluse. Why don't we see a movie tomorrow night? Unless you have other plans?"

"Why, no," Melanie replied, apparently pleased with the invitation. "There's a new Kevin Costner film playing at the Royal that I've been wanting to see. Do you like him?"

"Are you kidding? What red-blooded American woman doesn't? I'll even spring for the popcorn."

"Buttered?"

Alex grinned and consigned a week's extra calories to oblivion. "Do they serve it any other way?"

"Right. And if you drink a diet soda with it, the calories don't count."

Alex was starting to like Melanie more all the time. "That's always been my theory."

The others rejoined them then, and Alex left with her housemates. They chatted pleasantly during the brief ride home, and it wasn't long before they all declared themselves ready to retire for the evening.

As they were turning out the lights, Dottie said, "Oh, Alex, I almost forgot. Johnnie Mae and Mildred and I are going to a concert by the high school orchestra to-morrow night. Johnnie Mae's niece is playing in it. Would you like to join us?"

Alex declined politely, suppressing a smile of antic-ipation. "I'd love to, but I've already made plans for tomorrow evening."

Dottie's eyes lit up.

Mildred frowned. "Plans?" she asked, typically the first to do so. "What plans?"

"I'm going to a movie with Melanie."

"You and Melanie have a date?" Johnnie Mae asked, grinning as she glanced at the other two.

Alex chuckled. "I certainly wouldn't call it a date. Just two friends, spending an evening together."

She headed for her room then, leaving Dottie biting her lip against a rueful smile and Mildred shaking her head and muttering beneath her breath.

AFTER SPENDING several hours touring a grain eleva-tor—another site to be utilized in her book—Alex re-turned early Saturday afternoon to find the house empty, her hostesses all out, occupied with their usual busy routines. She rather enjoyed the solitude for a while; it gave her a chance to type up her notes while they were still fresh in her mind. She pulled one of her diet colas out of the refrigerator, her thoughts filled with plot possibilities that had occurred to her during her research tour.

She'd already decided the grain elevator made a ter-rific location for the murder that would occur early in the novel, the one her private investigator—one of the strong, capable, independent women Alex so enjoyed creating—would be called upon to look into. At the risk of her life, of course. She planned, as well, to incorporate many of the experiences she'd had in this rural area; she envisioned her heroine as another, out-of-her-element city girl. She told herself it was only a natural story development for the love interest to be the local, small-town doctor. He wouldn't be at all like Kane, of course. Maybe he'd have green eyes.

When she found the jacket she'd worn the evening before still draped over the back of the desk chair, she remembered how thoroughly she'd enjoyed her evening with Melanie at the movies. As if by unspoken agreement, neither of them had mentioned Kane, keeping their conversation light and humorous, discussing their work, their tastes in books, music and movies, current fashions and politics.

Alex had really needed the diversion, and had been able to relax and savor the companionship of another woman closer to her own age than her sweet, but sometimes perplexing, hostesses. And she'd managed not to think about Kane for most of the evening, though he'd popped into her thoughts quite annoyingly, when she was least prepared.

Just as she was suddenly thinking of him now. She closed her eyes for a moment and found herself back on the lawn swing, Kane's arms around her, his lips moving on hers. She quickly opened her eyes again and turned with grim determination to her work.

Kane had made no effort to be alone with her again since that interlude Monday evening, so she was obviously wasting her time, agonizing over whether she should allow herself to become involved with him while

she was in town. He'd obviously agreed with her that
doing so would be foolish, a mistake for both of them.

She managed to lose herself quite satisfactorily in her
work, then the phone rang. Sighing, she thought of
letting it ring, and wished for a moment that Dottie had
an answering machine. But she cleared her computer
screen and picked up the extension on her bedside table.

"Oh, Alex, I'm so glad you're home!"

"Dottie? Is something wrong?" Alex asked, concerned at Dottie's rather frantic tone.

"No, nothing serious. It's just that we've been held
up here at the church. You know, our fall bazaar is only
two weeks away, and suddenly everything's in chaos,
and it looks like we're going to be here several more
hours, and I've already asked Kane to join us for dinner tonight. I simply won't have time to prepare anything. I hate to ask you this, dear, but do you think you
could help me out?"

Having followed the rambling explanation with some
difficulty, Alex gulped. "You want *me* to make dinner?" she asked weakly.

"I'd really appreciate it. Unless you'd rather not, of
course," Dottie added, her voice falling to a near sigh.
"In that case, I'll just call Kane and tell him we'll have
to make it another night."

"Oh, Dottie, I'd like to help you out. It's just that I'm
really not much of a cook. I wasn't kidding when I said
I could hardly boil water."

"Oh. Well, then I suppose I'll call Kane—"

"No." Alex wasn't sure why she was so suddenly reluctant for Dottie to call her son and cancel his dinner

invitation, just because she herself couldn't put a meal together. "I'll—I'll come up with something, Dottie. Don't worry about it."

Dottie's tone brightened noticeably. "You really don't mind?"

"Not at all. It's the least I can do after you've been so nice to me."

"Oh, Alex, thank you. I was sure you could handle this." Dottie sounded oddly smug. "We'll be home around six. Kane's due to arrive about the same time."

"I'll have everything ready," Alex promised rashly.

"Thank you, dear. You're a lifesaver. I have to go now. See you this evening."

"All right." Alex hung up the telephone with a groan.

She was preparing dinner for five? To be served in less than two hours? Had she lost her mind? Did she really think Dottie and Kane—not to mention Mildred—would be content with grilled cheese sandwiches and canned tomato soup, Alex's one and only, totally edible menu?

She knew what she would have done in this situation in Chicago, of course. She snatched up the telephone book in desperation, only to learn that her hostesses hadn't been exaggerating when they'd told her that Andersenville had extremely limited take-out services. Pizza was the only choice. And Alex would really hate to see poor Johnnie Mae break out in splotches after dinner.

She groaned again and headed for the kitchen, hoping to find something—anything—that looked quick, easy and appetizing.

Unfortunately, Dottie and her friends weren't into fast food and quickie entrées. Dottie was the cook-from-scratch type; she even turned her nose up at canned biscuits and cake mixes, and the pantry was stocked with cooking basics. Dottie didn't use recipes much, either, but there were a couple of cookbooks stuffed in the back of the pantry. Alex glared at them and wondered what the odds were that she could follow directions, just this once, without messing up, especially considering the limited time she had to work with.

Why hadn't any eager, young entrepreneurs recognized the potential for a good delivery service in Andersenville? she moaned in frustration.

Eager young entrepreneurs. She caught her breath and looked hopefully at the telephone, suddenly struck by a brilliant idea. Maybe . . .

Seconds later, she spoke into the receiver in her warmest, friendliest, most gracious, author-to-fan tone. "Tommy? Hi, it's Alexandra Bennett. I have a problem and I was really hoping you could help me out . . ."

8

As it happened, the ladies and Kane arrived for dinner at almost exactly the same time. Taking only a moment to check that her garnet silk blouse was neatly tucked into the waistband of her coordinating print skirt, Alex opened the door with a smile of welcome. "Did everything work out at the church?" she asked, reaching for Dottie's coat.

Dottie nodded and eyed Alex in question. "We made quite a bit of progress, though there's still a great deal to do before next weekend. Mmm . . . Did everything work out here?"

"Oh, yes. I got quite a lot of work done today."

Kane shrugged out of his jacket and gave Alex a nod of greeting, his expression carefully neutral. "Something smells really good in the kitchen," he commented.

"Yes, it does," Mildred agreed, thin eyebrows lifted. "Obviously you exaggerated about your lack of culinary talent, Alex."

Alex laughed and shook her head. "No, trust me, I didn't. But I like to think I'm the resourceful type in an emergency," she added, leading the others into the dining room, where the table was set with Dottie's best dishes around a centerpiece of fresh flowers and candles Alex had wheedled a local florist into sending over at extremely short notice.

"Oh, Alex, everything looks lovely!" Johnnie Mae enthused, settling into her chair in anticipation. "I'm starving," she added eagerly.

"Hmm. You're always hungry," Mildred rebuked her, with a meaningful look at Johnnie Mae's ample figure.

Johnnie Mae glanced just as emphatically at Mildred's bony frame. "Well, not everyone can eat all they want and stay skinny as a rail."

Dottie interceded quickly. "Do you need any help in the kitchen, Alex?"

Alex shook her head. "You've put in a long day. Let me take care of everything now. Please, Dottie, have a seat, and I'll serve the salad."

Knowing Kane was watching her with a quizzical half smile, Alex turned and hurried into the kitchen, oddly nervous in her role as hostess. Why did she suddenly feel as though she was being tested again? And why did it really matter, if she was?

She'd made the salad herself. After all, even she was capable of chopping up fresh vegetables and tossing them with a light, vinaigrette dressing. Even Mildred seemed to enjoy the salad, though she couldn't seem to resist murmuring that salad was certainly easy enough to prepare.

Everyone seemed eager to discover what Alex would produce for a main course. She held her breath as she carried in the steaming dishes, fresh from the warming oven. Glazed ham. Candied yams. Turnip greens. Black-eyed peas. She had once heard Mildred describe her favorite meal. A coconut pie, piled high with fluffy meringue, waited in the kitchen. Mildred's favorite dessert. Alex had known all along who'd be her toughest critic.

Dottie's eyes rounded comically. "How in the world . . . ?"

Mildred was already filling her plate. "This sure looks good. But I don't know how you managed it," she added. "You certainly didn't have time to bake a ham since Dottie called you."

"No," Alex admitted. "I told you, I'm good at improvising."

Kane suddenly laughed. "It's the Friday night special from Kelley's Diner," he said as his mother clapped her hands in delight at Alex's cleverness. "Now, how did you manage to sweet-talk Hank Kelley into preparing a take-out meal for you?"

Alex returned his grin with a touch of pride. "Actually, I sweet-talked Tommy. He wants to be a writer, you know."

She tried not to think how much the dinner had cost her, with the more than generous delivery fees and tips for the florist and Tommy. At the moment, it seemed worth every dollar she'd spent.

Kane's gaze lingered on her smiling mouth. "Anyone ever tell you that you're a dangerous woman, Alexandra Bennett?"

She swallowed and chose not to answer that one. "Would you like some ham, Kane?" she asked instead.

"Are you kidding? I'm ravenous. And everything looks great. I—oh, hell."

The annoying beeping drew sighs from everyone at the table. "Poor Kane," Johnnie Mae murmured, glancing up from the yams she'd just piled onto her plate.

"I suppose you have to answer that," Dottie sighed, gazing regretfully from Kane to Alex.

"Yeah, I'm afraid so." Kane rose reluctantly, sparing one longing look at the food on the table. "I'm sorry, Alex. I know you went to a lot of trouble for this."

"It's not your fault," Alex assured him. "I'm only sorry you didn't have a chance to eat."

"I'm used to it." He watched her as he spoke, donning the jacket he'd tossed over the back of his chair just a moment ago.

"Yes. I know," she returned, aware that he was subtly reminding her, yet again, of the demands of his job.

She told herself that it was only coincidence that Kane hadn't been called away from the meal Melanie had prepared earlier that week.

He could hardly be blamed for the poor timing of a medical emergency, no matter how much Alex might be tempted to do so.

KANE'S DEPARTURE took some of the pleasure out of the meal, but Alex and the others made an effort to enjoy it, anyway. They kept a lively conversation going as they cleaned their plates. Afterward, Dottie, Mildred and Johnnie Mae insisted on helping with the clearing away, even though Alex tried to persuade them to allow her to take care of that, too.

Nearly two hours after they'd finished dinner, Alex was watching a television musical special with Mildred and Johnnie Mae, when Dottie joined them. "I just saw

Kane drive into his garage," she announced, looking at Alex as she spoke.

"I hope he had a chance to eat something," Johnnie Mae fretted, drawing her attention away from the television screen.

Dottie was still looking at Alex. "Maybe one of us should take him a plate of leftovers from dinner."

The message couldn't have been clearer if Dottie had held up a cue card. Alex bit her lip against a smile at the less-than-subtle hint. "Would you like me to take him something, Dottie?"

Dottie did a fairly creditable job of looking pleasantly surprised that Alex had "volunteered." "Why, thank you, dear. I'm sure Kane will appreciate it."

Alex wasn't about to try to second-guess Kane's reaction. As far as she was concerned, she was simply taking him his dinner. She'd play it by ear after that.

Dottie piled enough food upon a tray to feed several starving doctors, then set the tray in a basket. "No need to hurry back," she assured Alex. "Since you passed on dessert earlier, I've put in an extra slice of coconut pie for you. Kane will probably enjoy your company. He eats alone so often, you know."

Alex was growing increasingly uncomfortable with Dottie's blatant manipulation. "Dottie . . ." she began, unsure whether to be flattered or alarmed that Kane's mother was all but pushing her into Kane's arms.

The older woman held up both hands. "That's all. I promise."

"Thank you. Is this everything?"

"Yes. Watch your step crossing the yard. Mildred found a gopher hole earlier."

"I will. Thanks."

Dottie opened the back door for her, then closed it firmly behind her when she stepped outside.

Alex stood on the doorstep for a moment, eyes focused on the lights in Kane's windows; she briefly wished she'd taken time to put on a sweater. The temperature had dropped considerably since she'd been out earlier. She shivered.

It occurred to her as she pressed Kane's doorbell that she'd never been inside his house. She wondered if it would be decorated like his mother's in comfortable, Early American, or whether it would be a more typical mélange of bachelor furnishings.

She knew the wisest course of action would be to bolt back to the safety of Dottie's house, if he invited her inside. She knew just as well that she wouldn't.

Kane opened the door. "Alex. Is anything wrong?"

At the sight of him, she temporarily lost her voice. His dark coffee-colored hair tumbled onto his forehead, accentuating the roguish charm of a day's growth of beard. His feet were bare beneath the ragged hems of faded jeans that rode low on his lean hips. His chest was bare—gloriously bare—furred with a light dusting of dark hair. He hadn't taken time to put on the gray sweatshirt he was holding in one hand.

Alex was tempted to throw the heavy basket behind her and attack him on the spot. She'd never seen anyone more devastatingly appealing than Dr. Kane Lovell, caught relaxing in the privacy of his home.

"Alex?" he prompted, frowning at her silence.

She forced her voice through dry lips. "I...er...your mother thought you might be hungry. I brought dinner."

He smiled and glanced at the basket in her white-knuckled hands. "Thank you. She was right, I'm starving. I was just about to raid the refrigerator for whatever I could find."

Sternly reminding herself that this was hardly the first time she'd seen a man without his shirt—never mind that Kane had the most gorgeous chest she'd ever seen in her life—Alex held out the basket. "Why don't you raid this instead?"

"Hold on a second." He tugged the sweatshirt over his head, then straightened his hair with a sweep of his fingers. "Now I'm a little more fit for company," he said, taking the basket. "Would you like to come in?"

Now was the time to bolt. Instead, Alex nodded, moistening her lips with the tip of her tongue. "Yes, I'd like that. For a little while," she added cautiously.

"Oh, this is nice," she said a moment later, looking around as she followed Kane through a large den.

She'd guessed wrong about his decor. Kane's house was done with a Southwestern motif, in light woods and woven fabrics of blue, coral, beige and off-white. Western landscapes were cleverly grouped on the painted walls, and hand-thrown pottery decorated the low tables that were scattered among the comfortably arranged couches and chairs. Authentic-looking Native American rugs dotted the wooden floors. Hopi? Navajo? Alex couldn't be sure, though she identified the collection of Hopi kachina dolls in a corner curio cabinet. Built-in bookcases on either side of a natural stone fireplace held Remington cowboy sculptures.

"I take it you hired a professional decorator," she said, thinking how much more polished his house looked than the hodgepodge of furnishings she'd collected for her apartment in Chicago.

"No, but thanks for the compliment," Kane replied, pushing through a swinging saloon door leading into the kitchen. "I decorated it myself."

Alex was already admiring the huge, airy kitchen with its hanging, copper-bottomed pots, bleached wooden cabinets and blue and coral-tiled countertops. "Kane, this is lovely. You really designed it all yourself?"

He shrugged a bit self-consciously and placed the heavy basket upon a convenient work island. "I needed something to do when I'm not working. I've spent the past two years haunting furniture stores and art galleries. I've finished the den, dining room, kitchen and master bedroom, but I've still got an empty living room and three empty bedrooms to furnish eventually."

A four-bedroom house for a bachelor? It was obvious that Kane hadn't intended to live alone for long. Had he designed his home with his former fiancée in mind? Had he hoped to find someone soon to replace her in his life? Maybe the three, dear little matchmakers next door had acted with his full approval in introducing him to Melanie—and to the other young women they'd mentioned during Alex's stay.

Maybe Dottie was hoping that Alex would be the one to share this beautiful house with her son. Dottie couldn't know, of course, that Alex would give anything to share a home and a life with someone—as long as she could be sure the someone she chose could give her the unqualified love and attention she'd spent a lifetime longing for.

"There's enough food in here for an army," Kane said, unpacking the basket. "Would you like something?"

"I'll have dessert with you after you've eaten. How about if I make some coffee to go with it?"

"Sounds good. Everything's in the cabinet to the right of the sink." He carried a well-filled plate to the small, round, oak table that stood in a deep, glass bay window, overlooking the sweeping, back lawn.

It suddenly seemed very quiet in the kitchen as Alex prepared the coffee. Spotting a radio built into the wall beneath the cabinets, she reached for it, then hesitated. "Do you mind if I turn on some music?"

"Feel free. Anything but rap, please."

She laughed. "I think that can be arranged." She turned the dial until she found a station that played mellow, contemporary music, leaving the volume low. Just enough to take the edge off the silence. "How's that?"

"Fine." He looked up from his meal to smile at her. "It's nice having you here, Alex. I've been wondering what it would take to get you here."

She leaned against the countertop behind her and watched him eat. "You were only gone a few hours. I assume it wasn't a terrible emergency?" Though she wasn't sure how much he could tell her about his work, it seemed a safer subject than the one he'd skirted.

Kane shook his head. "One of my elderly patients, who's been hospitalized for the past week, gave us a scare tonight. He's stable now. I'm pretty sure it was a reaction to a new medication we were trying. I took him off it and left instructions for the nurses to call me, if there are any further developments tonight."

"So you could be leaving again before you even drink your coffee."

He nodded, his expression sober. "Yeah. For him—for someone else. I'm on call tonight. If I'm needed, I'll go."

Her smile felt strained. "No wonder doctors have so much trouble with their personal lives."

"It's certainly not for everyone. But I can't imagine ever doing anything else."

Nor could Alex imagine anyone ever asking him to do anything else. Kane belonged here, was needed here. And his unselfish dedication to his patients was as appealing as it was intimidating.

Maybe this wasn't such a safe subject, after all. "How's the food?" she asked instead.

Kane lifted an eyebrow at the abrupt change of topic, but went along. "It's great. That was very clever of you to find a way to provide dinner so quickly. Impressed the hell out of Aunt Mildred."

Alex shrugged. "I'm sure Melanie could have whipped up a gourmet meal with a couple of potatoes and a pinch of basil, but this was the best I could do on such short notice."

"Hey, it worked out. That's all that counts." He swallowed the last bite of his dinner and pushed the plate away. "Did you say something about joining me for dessert?"

"Coconut pie. Ready for yours?"

"You bet. Are you going to sit down with me now, or do you plan to eat standing up at that counter?" His tone was amused, yet understanding.

Alex swallowed a groan at her uncharacteristically awkward behavior. She wished she knew what it was about Kane that turned her from a competent, confident, professional woman to a shy, nervous idiot.

Kane didn't say anything until they'd almost finished their desserts. Then he asked casually, "So, have you heard from your boyfriend in Chicago lately?"

Alex choked and swallowed frantically. That was one question she really hadn't been expecting! To be honest, she couldn't even remember the last time Bill had crossed her mind.

"I . . . er . . . haven't talked to him in a few days."

"That doesn't bother you? Or him?"

"No, of course not. Why should it?"

Kane slanted her a look through his lashes as he sliced into the last of his pie. "It would sure as hell bother me—if you belonged to me, of course."

Alex forced a smile. "Watch it, Kane. You're starting to sound a bit dated with that talk of 'belonging' to someone."

"In case you haven't noticed, I've got a few old-fashioned tendencies. And I'm not sure I'd like the woman in my life going off for weeks at a time, with no word about where she is or what she's doing. Or who she's doing it with," he added reflectively.

Alex had suddenly lost what little appetite she'd had. She pushed away the remainder of her dessert. "And here I've been thinking you're a progressive, modern male," she said, trying to sound as though she was teasing.

"I think you could bring out the primitive instincts inside any man, Alex. So I can't help wondering why a man who's asked you to marry him would risk having a man like me try to take you away from him."

It was beginning to look as though she should have bolted, after all. "Kane, I—"

"I haven't stopped wanting you, Alex. I've tried to give you time, but I'm afraid I'm running out of will-power. I want you until it's getting damned hard for me to think of anything else."

She clenched her hands in her lap, drawn to the sincerity in his deep voice. It was a heady feeling to be wanted by this man, despite her caution about getting involved unwisely.

If only she could enjoy being with him and still find the strength to walk away, rather than take second place to his other responsibilities.... If only she could believe she wouldn't be leaving her heart behind when she went!

Though she kept her eyes focused intently on her hands, she heard the scraping of Kane's chair on the tile floor. A moment later he knelt beside her, his large, tanned hand coming into focus as it covered her icy fingers. "Alex?"

She forced her gaze upward. His hazel eyes were so intent as they stared into hers. His beautifully shaped mouth so temptingly close to her own. It was very hard to think of all the obstacles that stood between them, when she had only to move a few inches to be in his arms.

Kane waited patiently, so quiet and still that she could almost hear her own, frantic heartbeat over the soft music still playing from the radio. His eyes held hers, his hand was firm on her own, but she knew full well that he'd release her without hesitation, if she asked.

She couldn't ask.

A trembling sigh escaped her parted lips. "Kane," she whispered, lifting a hand to his cheek. "Please . . ."

He didn't make it necessary for her to finish the request. His mouth was on hers before she could say another word, whatever it might have been. Alex closed her eyes and wrapped her arms around his neck, consigning common sense to the devil, at least for tonight.

As though he sensed she'd made her choice, Kane groaned and rose, pulling her out of the chair and into his arms, holding her so tightly that she could feel the fine tremor running through the solid muscles. His kiss changed from something skilled and persuasive to a rough, greedy caress. And Alex realized for the first time exactly how badly Kane wanted her.

He'd masked his need before, kept his desire under strict control in deference to her misgivings. Now he held nothing back, putting everything he felt, everything he wanted into an embrace that nearly melted her spine. And Alex responded to his passion with a fiery intensity she'd never known before, a hunger as deep and raw as his kiss.

He muttered something incoherent against her lips and swung her high against his chest before she could protest. Her arms tightened reflexively around his neck as he turned and strode swiftly out of the kitchen. She'd never been carried to bed before, never fantasized about being swept along by mindless, even primitive passion. Yet she found herself reveling in Kane's strength, content for the first time in her life to feel small and feminine against a man's size and virility.

Maybe she'd be embarrassed later that she'd allowed herself to be seduced so effortlessly, but for now she chose to savor the experience.

When they reached his bedroom, Kane lowered her slowly to her feet beside the massive bed, his eyes locked with hers.

Without saying anything, he reached out to turn on a small bedside lamp and then snapped off the overhead light, so that the room was cast into soft, cozy shadow. Alex kicked off her flats, her bare feet sinking into the luxurious, bedroom carpet as she waited with held breath for Kane to turn back to her.

She bit her lip when he cupped her face between his large, surprisingly gentle hands. "You're so beautiful," he murmured, his eyes caressing her features.

Alex knew she wasn't classically beautiful; she was attractive, at most. She'd decided years ago it wasn't really important. But now she trembled in pleasure at Kane's words, at the sincerity in his deep, rough-edged voice. She wanted to be beautiful to him, probably because Kane was so utterly beautiful in her eyes.

He touched his lips to her forehead, ruffling the dark curls there with his warm breath. She closed her eyes, curling her fingers into his soft sweatshirt.

His lips touched her eyelids and she could feel his smile. The faintest of kisses on the tip of her nose made her smile in return, though she didn't open her eyes.

As he brushed his lips against her cheek, she arched into him like a cat, hungry for more of his touch.

He slid his open palms slowly down her back, his skin warm through the thin silk of her blouse. "Tell me you want me."

"Yes." The word was little more than a sigh.

"Tell me."

"I want you."

"Alex." He crushed her mouth beneath his, no longer gentle or teasing. She wouldn't have complained, had he given her the chance.

Her blouse closed with a single button at the nape. He found and released that button, then tugged the hem from the waistband of her skirt. Alex raised her arms to allow him to pull the blouse over her head. He released another button, and her skirt fell to tangle around her bare feet, leaving her clad only in a slinky, flesh-colored, silk and lace teddy.

Alex's cheeks warmed. She usually wore more practical underclothing. Had she subconsciously planned for the evening to end this way?

Murmuring his pleasure, Kane stroked his hands from her throat to her hips, pausing to cup her breasts in his palms, to span her slender waist with his fingers. Alex stood still, her hands clenched at her sides, basking in his sensual admiration, burning wherever he touched her. And then his hands were at her shoulders again, and the tiny, spaghetti straps of her teddy were brushed out of the way. The garment fell to her hips.

"Alex." Kane's voice was thick, disturbed, his gaze hot on her sensitive, hard-tipped breasts. "My God,

Alex, you're perfect." He reached out to pull the teddy down her legs, his mouth seeking hers again.

Alex tipped back her head and gave herself wholly to the kiss, trembling at the sensation of being nude in his arms, his clothing brushing her sensitized skin. The room was cool, and a breeze from somewhere skimmed over her back. She shivered in aroused response. She'd never been more deeply aware of her own sexuality. To think she'd often wondered what all the fuss was about!

Remembering how Kane had looked when he'd answered the door without his shirt, Alex was suddenly impatient with the fabric between them now. She reached for the hem of his sweatshirt, and Kane helped her remove it. The difference in their height put his nipples within easy reach of her mouth. She touched the tip of her tongue to one tiny point and was rewarded by his sharp inhale.

"You're the beautiful one, Kane," she said artlessly, smiling up at him.

He groaned and pressed her into the bed beside them, reaching for the snap of his jeans even as he followed her down. "I've never wanted anyone like this," he muttered, his mouth at her breast. "I've never needed anyone this badly. God, Alex, what are you doing to me?"

She couldn't answer. She could only arch helplessly upward when he tugged her deeply, firmly into his mouth, the movements of his lips and tongue drawing a faint cry from her throat. She was aching, swollen, hot, and the clever hand he slid between her legs offered only partial satisfaction. She wanted more, needed more, longed to feel him so deep inside that he'd never want to leave her, could never be taken away from her.

With a desperation that was new to her, she rolled with him across the bed, her hands as wild, as greedy as his, her mouth as hungry, as avid. Neither of them could say a coherent word, so they spoke through skillful touches and deep, wet kisses, through broken murmurs and ragged sighs.

Kane's breath heaved from his chest; he fumbled with a foil package, uncharacteristically clumsy, cursing beneath his breath for a moment, before returning eagerly to her waiting arms. Alex's heart pounded frantically in her chest as he settled between her legs. Even as she shifted to accommodate him, she wondered dimly if she was making a terrible mistake.

She knew without doubt that her life was about to change permanently. She would never be the same after tonight. It seemed she had little choice. She'd wanted Kane Lovell from the night she'd stumbled into his arms, only a week and a half ago.

As though sensing her sudden doubts, Kane hesitated, on the verge of bringing them together. "Alex?" he whispered through tightly held lips, his entire body quivering with the restraint he held himself under. "Do you want me to stop?"

"No. Oh, no," she assured him, tugging at his shoulders with feverish hands. Whatever the consequences, she thought she'd die if he stopped now.

His eyelids closed just for a moment in sheer relief, then lifted again so that he could watch her as he suddenly surged forward.

Alex stiffened and cried out, momentary discomfort rapidly replaced by sheer pleasure. Nothing had ever felt more right, nothing more glorious. "Kane! Oh, Kane."

"Alex. Alex, I—" He broke off with a groan when she moved sinuously against him. "Oh, God."

And then he was moving with her, and neither of them could speak at all. The explosion of sensations that rocked Alex a moment later tore a broken, startled cry from her throat. Her body stiffened sharply into an arc that brought her half off the bed, before Kane pressed her downward with his own muffled growl of satisfaction.

Limp, dazed, bemused, Alex lay in his arms for a long time afterward, refusing to allow herself to think of the future. Her cheek cradled in the hollow of his shoulder, she rested a hand on his chest and concentrated on counting the heartbeats beneath her palm, pleased that it took a while for his rapid pulse to slow. She wasn't the only one who'd been overwhelmed by the powerful intensity of their lovemaking.

She knew it was growing late, that she really should make herself dress and go back to her room next door. But, oh, how she hated the thought of leaving Kane's arms! She sighed and started to rise, deciding it was now or never.

Kane's arm tightened around her. "Where are you going?"

"It's getting late. I'd better go."

He drew his thumb across her swollen lower lip. "Stay with me tonight." His voice was deep, persuasive.

She wanted nothing more than to settle back into his arms and hold reality at bay for a few more hours. But . . . "What about your mother?" she asked doubtfully.

Kane lifted an eyebrow. "What about her?"

"What will she think if I stay?"

His mouth crooked upward at the corner, deepening the dimple in his cheek. "That you had a good time?" he hazarded teasingly, tugging at one of the curls tumbled around her face.

"Kane," Alex chided. "You know what I mean."

"We're adults, Alex. Neither of us has to explain our actions to my mother."

"But won't she think—?"

"Alex," he interrupted. "My mother has nothing to do with this. Do you want to stay or not?"

She sighed. "Yes."

"Then c'mere," he ordered, pulling her more firmly into his arms. "Damn, I'm tired. D'you mind if we sleep for a while and talk later?"

"No," she murmured, snuggling her cheek back into his shoulder. "I don't mind at all."

She wasn't ready to talk, wasn't ready to face the real world. For now she needed the fantasy. She closed her eyes and allowed herself to drift off to sleep, carrying the illusions with her into her dreams.

SHE COULDN'T HAVE SAID how many hours had passed when Kane woke her. But again, talk was the furthest thing from their minds as his hands swept her body, guiding her so easily back into the passion they'd found before.

Alex was thrilled that the ecstasy she'd known with him hadn't been a onetime experience. Their lovemaking was as intensely satisfying the second time as it had been before. Somehow she knew it would always be this perfect with Kane. Just as she suspected it would never be as good with anyone else.

"Alex," Kane moaned, moments after they climaxed, together, with muffled shouts of satisfaction that still echoed in the dark corners of the quiet bedroom. "Stay with me. Not just for tonight. Don't go back to Chicago."

Her breath was still coming in ragged gasps, her breasts were heaving beneath him. "Kane, please," she whispered, covering his mouth with a trembling hand. "Not tonight. Not yet."

He caught her hand in his, pressing a hot, open-mouthed kiss onto her palm. "All right," he agreed roughly. "Not tonight. But soon. Tomorrow."

She didn't answer, but drew his head down to hers for another long, thorough kiss. And by the time they finally fell asleep again, neither of them had the energy to talk—or even think—about tomorrow.

9

ALEX FROWNED and stirred restlessly, gradually becoming aware that there was light against her eyelids and something hard and lumpy in her bed. She squirmed again, trying to get comfortable. Failing. Something was digging painfully into her back.

Reaching beneath her without opening her eyes, she closed her fingers around what felt like hard, cool plastic. She held it up and reluctantly opened her eyes, squinting against the sunlight coming through a nearby window. A pager, she thought blankly, staring in confusion at the small, black box in her hand. What was a pager doing in her bed?

No. Not her bed. *Kane's* bed.

Fully awake now, she gasped and sat upright, the sheets falling to her waist as she looked around. She was alone in the room, but she could hear a shower running in the adjoining bathroom.

Memories of the night before flooded her mind, making her catch her breath and close her eyes for a moment. She'd never known any night could be that perfect, that beautiful.

That terrifying.

"Stay with me. Not just for tonight. Don't go back to Chicago."

She opened her eyes quickly to make sure the words had only been in her head. They'd sounded so clear that she wouldn't have been too surprised to find Kane standing at the foot of the bed, repeating them. But the shower was still running, and she could hear him humming a lively tune over the sound of the water. And she panicked.

Throwing the pager onto the nightstand, she snatched her clothing from the floor and jerked them on, not taking particular care with buttons or zippers. Her heart pounded as though she was about to be caught robbing a house or something. Even though she knew she was being foolish, she still had to get away before Kane came back into the room.

She barely took time to slide her feet into her shoes before she left, running across the morning-dewed lawn and into the house next door, without giving herself time to think about what she was doing.

Alex was fervently grateful that none of her housemates were in the kitchen when she slipped through the back door. The house was still quiet. She knew it was their habit to sleep a bit later than usual on Sunday mornings, giving themselves just enough time to have a quick breakfast and dress for church. She intended to be gone when they came downstairs.

In her room, she changed into jeans and a sweater, tied on a pair of running shoes, thinking ironically that they were an appropriate choice of footwear, and scribbled a note for Dottie, explaining that she'd be spending the day doing more research, so she shouldn't look for her anytime soon. And then she escaped, sliding behind the wheel of the rented car and driving away with no destination in mind, just the certainty that she needed time alone. Time to think, time to make some decisions, time to try to analyze her complex, utterly bewildering feelings for Kane Lovell.

Time to try to convince herself that she hadn't really fallen helplessly, permanently, desperately in love with a man who already belonged to the rest of the world.

KANE RAN OUT his front door, just in time to see Alex's car disappear down the road, heading away from Andersenville. "Damn," he growled, fighting an urge to leap into his own car and give chase. "Dammit, Alex."

He didn't really have to ask why she'd run. Perhaps he'd half expected her to do so.

He'd sensed her panic when he'd asked her to stay with him in a weak moment of vulnerability during the night. He should have waited, should have known it was too soon to make requests like that. But the thought of her going back to another man, after being in his arms, had made him reckless.

Whether she was willing to admit it or not, Alex was his now. And Kane had no intention of standing meekly aside if she tried to leave.

He'd given up on love before, had watched another woman walk away, and it had nearly torn him apart. This time he wasn't sure he would survive.

He'd loved Cathy with the rather naive enthusiasm of youth, the rosy optimism of hot-blooded infatuation. His feelings for Alex were those of a full grown man, who'd found the one woman he wanted for his mate. And in the way of men since the beginning of time, Kane was prepared to fight for her, if necessary.

So Alex could run for today, if she needed to. She could try to convince herself that what they'd shared had been nothing more than a temporary fling, if she liked.

But Kane had felt her come apart in his arms, had recognized the startled discovery in her eyes, when she'd lost herself in passion. He knew what had passed between them had been as wondrous for Alex as it had been for him. That she'd never experienced anything like it with anyone else, just as he hadn't. He was willing to give her a little time to recognize those truths.

Not much time. He wasn't that noble. He was already impatient to hold her again, to love her again. And he didn't know how long he'd be able to wait for her to come to him on her own.

Exhaling gustily, he stepped back into his house and closed the door. Though it was Sunday, he had early rounds to make at the hospital, patients to check on. He knew exactly why Alex worried about getting involved with a man with his responsibilities, especially since she'd told him about her parents. He sympathized with her misgivings—and fully understood them.

Yes, he'd give her a little time. Time to realize for herself that it was already too late to pull back. That the emotions that had flared between them were strong enough to overcome all the odds against them, if only they were both willing to work at overcoming those odds.

Kane was willing. Now all he had to do was convince Alex that what they could have was worth the effort.

"SHE DIDN'T COME HOME last night." Dottie made the announcement with satisfaction.

Johnnie Mae's eyes widened. "You're sure?"

"I'm positive. And we all know where she was."

Mildred scowled. "Hmm. Just because she and Kane fooled around last night doesn't mean they're going to get married. That's probably just the way young people carry on all the time in Chicago."

"Why, Mildred! You know very well that Alex is a nice young woman. And my son isn't the sort to indulge in one-night stands. You've seen the way he looks at Alex. He's completely taken with her."

"Doesn't mean she feels the same way," Mildred argued. "There's still that man in Chicago."

Dottie sighed. "I know. I wish I knew exactly what was going on between the two of them. But surely Alex would mention him occasionally, if she really cared for him, wouldn't she? I mean, she hasn't even called him, other than the one time, to let him know where she would be staying."

Johnnie Mae was wringing her hands. "I just can't bear it if she hurts Kane. It about broke my heart when Cathy dumped him, the way she did. Kane's too soft-hearted. He doesn't deserve to be hurt the way Cathy hurt him—the way Alex could hurt him, if she doesn't feel the same way about him that he apparently feels about her."

"I think she does care for Kane," Dottie said thoughtfully, though she frowned at the reminder of how deeply Kane had suffered after the breakup of his engagement. "She's just understandably concerned, because it's happening so quickly, and because she's aware that Kane's job is one that's going to require a great deal of understanding and patience from his wife. You saw how disappointed she was, when he had to leave before we could have dinner last night. It's only natural that she would wonder if she can deal with that, all the time."

"And if she decides she can't?" Mildred demanded.

Dottie shrugged. "I don't know. I only hope Kane can convince her that he's worth the effort."

"Any girl would have to be a fool not to know that," Johnnie Mae said loyally.

"You can bet *Melanie* knows it." Mildred nodded her gray head, as if to emphasize her defiant challenge.

"Mildred, if Kane were interested in Melanie, he'd have asked her out long before this," Dottie pointed out impatiently.

"He's just been bedazzled by Alex. After all, she is quite different from the women he's used to around here. But you mark my words, he'll come to his senses. He'll see that he needs a different kind of woman. One who can make a home for him."

"She did manage to provide an excellent meal for us all, on very short notice," Johnnie Mae murmured, smiling at the memory.

"And she's made a lot of friends in the area," Dottie added. "She hasn't acted at all stuck-up or standoffish with the folks we've introduced her to."

"She even made a friend of Melanie," Johnnie Mae said with a laugh.

Mildred scowled. "Well, what about children, hmm? You know how badly Kane wants them. Melanie loves children. Alex probably wouldn't know what to do with a kid, if she had one. Those career-oriented, city women aren't interested in being mothers."

"You're generalizing again, Mildred. And how do you know that Alex wouldn't be wonderful with children?" Dottie demanded. "Look at how sweet and patient she's been with Tommy!"

"Tommy's half-grown. I'd like to see her with a houseful of kids. Bet she'd go running back to Chicago, faster than you could blink an eye."

Dottie lifted an eyebrow in a gesture that most people would have recognized as very like her son's. "You think so?"

"I'm positive."

Dottie smiled sweetly. "Then I guess we'll just have to see, won't we?"

Johnnie Mae eyed her friend suspiciously. "Dottie, what are you planning to do to Alex now?"

"Now don't you worry your head about it, Johnnie Mae. I know what I'm doing."

Johnnie Mae groaned. "That's what I'm afraid of. Those poor young people."

ALEX COULDN'T HAVE SAID exactly how she came to baby-sit three small, energetic children at Dottie's house Tuesday afternoon. Her hostess had manipulated her into watching the little dears, the children of a young neighbor with a dentist's appointment that afternoon.

Dottie had explained that she'd volunteered to watch the children herself, but had been called to the church to handle another crisis with the upcoming bazaar. And even though Alex had tried to explain that she'd never been responsible for small children in her entire life, somehow she ended up baby-sitting. Alone.

Alex took a deep breath. Three little faces looked expectantly up at her, clearly waiting for her to entertain them. "Er... what do you kids like to do for fun?"

Towheaded, five-year-old Rocky, the oldest of the Simpson brood, glanced at his three-year-old, copperhaired, twin sisters. "Casey likes to eat rocks. Kelly plays in the toilet. I like watching *Terminator* movies on cable. I think there's one playing now."

Since none of those activities seemed appropriate— Alex would be willing to bet that Polly Simpson never allowed Rocky to watch violent movies on cable—she realized she was going to have to come up with something else. "We could play a game."

Rocky looked bored. Kelly was inching toward the closest bathroom. "What game?" Casey asked, pushing her long, red bangs out of her round, blue eyes.

Thank goodness, the twins weren't identical, so Alex could tell them apart with a bit of concentration! She tried desperately to think of a game that might interest her charges.

Hide and seek? No. That would only give Kelly a chance to locate the nearest toilet.

Simon says? Probably too complicated for three-year-olds.

Poker? *Get real, Bennett.*

"Follow my leader," she suggested quickly, planting herself quickly between Kelly and the doorway.

"What's that?" Casey demanded, still the only one who looked particularly interested.

"I'll do something and you all do it, too. It'll be fun." Alex tried to sound more confident than she felt. "It's such a warm, beautiful afternoon. We'll go outside and play in the backyard." Maybe that way Dottie's house would be safe, on the off chance that the children got into the game just a bit too enthusiastically.

"What's the prize?" Rocky wanted to know.

"Prize?"

"Yeah. What does the winner get?"

"This really isn't that sort of game, Rocky. There are no winners or losers."

"Then why do you play?"

"For fun."

"Oh. *Terminator* movies are fun," he said reflectively. "Did you see the one where the bad guy stuck a knife right through—?"

Alex cut him off quickly, conscious of his little sisters listening avidly to big brother's gruesome tone. "Rocky, do your parents really allow you to watch those movies?"

He shuffled his feet and looked down at them. "Heather does."

"Who's Heather?"

"Our sometimes baby-sitter. She's in junior high," he added, looking impressed.

"Well, I'm not Heather, I'm Alex. And I think we should play a game now." She tried to speak with adult authority, then added, "I've already done junior high."

Rocky sighed, but agreed to try the game. Casey and Kelly were quickly persuaded to go along. Alex smiled, thinking that maybe this wouldn't be so difficult, after all.

Less than an hour later, she was ready to wave a white flag and surrender to the first adult she could find.

Alex was exhausted, Casey had fallen on the patio and scraped her knees, Rocky had disappeared into the den and had to be retrieved with some difficulty, and Kelly's shirt was wet to the elbows from a quick dip in the toilet, while Alex had disconnected the cable from the den television set. Alex had panicked, remembering stories she'd read about children drowning in toilets. She hadn't taken her eyes off Kelly since—which explained how Casey had managed to fall without Alex being close enough to catch her.

"Don't cry, Casey," she begged, cradling the sobbing child in her arms, while she kept one eye on the other two, who'd been ripping across the yard like tiny little dervishes when the accident occurred. "How about if we get a cookie or something?"

Casey's tears stopped magically. "A cookie?"

"Yeah. Sure. A cookie," Alex promised recklessly, praying their mother wasn't one of those health-conscious types who never allowed sweets.

Okay, so she knew she wasn't supposed to use food for a bribe or a reward, that it led to all sorts of horrible eating disorders in adolescence, that refined sugar was probably the root of juvenile delinquency. But she was desperate!

"Let's go into the kitchen and have some cookies and milk," she said brightly, assuring herself that at least the milk would be good for them.

Even Rocky seemed to think that was a good idea. "Got any choc'late chip?" he asked, crossing the patio to her side.

"I'm not sure, but we'll look. I know we have cookies, though. Mrs. Lovell bakes them herself."

"Miss Dottie makes good cookies," Casey agreed.

Alex pushed a limp curl out of her eyes and looked across the patio at the spot where Kelly leaned over the wrought iron railing, looking intently toward the woods at the far end of the sprawling lawn. "Kelly? Don't you want to go inside for a snack?"

Kelly glanced over her shoulder. "Cow."

Alex blinked. "What?"

"Saw a cow. Over there," Kelly added, pointing a chubby finger toward the woods.

Alex groaned. "Just what I needed to hear."

A deep, masculine laugh came from the kitchen doorway behind her. "Now you've got the kids doing it."

Alex's breath caught sharply in her throat at the sound of Kane's voice. Before she could stop it, her mind was filled with images of a darkened room, a big, soft bed and a warm, strong body pressed against hers. Feeling heat flood her face, she turned, self-consciously tucking a curl behind her ear. "Hello, Kane. What are you doing here?"

He shrugged, leaning against the doorjamb and looking so good her mouth went dry. In his eyes were reflections of the very memories that had set Alex's heart racing. "I had a couple of free hours and thought I'd drop by and see what was going on here. Er—what *is* going on here?"

She waved a hand to indicate the children around her. "I'm baby-sitting."

"Are you?" He smiled at Kelly, who'd walked up to him and stood staring expectantly upward, one finger in her mouth. "Where's Mother? She's usually the one who volunteers to watch Polly's kids."

"She had to go to the church. I got recruited."

Kane smiled as he took in her tumbled hair and grass-stained jeans. "So, how's it going?"

"How do *you* feel about children?" Alex asked in return, telling herself it wasn't, of course, a personal question. Merely curiosity.

"I like them," Kane answered, ruffling Rocky's hair.

"Good. Then you can join us for milk and cookies."

She turned as she spoke and marched toward the kitchen, trying to escape the heat in Kane's eyes. If he kept looking at her that way, there was no telling what she'd do, but she was certain it shouldn't be done in front of innocent children. She'd been expecting him to show up for an explanation, after considerately giving her a bit of time, but certainly hadn't expected him under these circumstances!

Casey showed Kane her scraped knees, while Alex poured milk and assembled homemade, chocolate chip cookies on paper plates. "Stay in here, please, Kelly," she said when she noticed the toddler inching toward the kitchen door. "Here, eat your cookies."

Kelly good-naturedly climbed into a chair and reached for her treat, seeming to accept the idea that Alex wasn't going to allow any more splashing for now.

After serving the children, Alex placed two large, soft cookies on a plate for Kane. She managed to keep her hand from shaking as she handed it to him—until his fingers brushed hers, obviously on purpose, when he took it. A tremor ran through her then, from her fingers to the soles of her feet. She swallowed a gasp and backed hastily out of range, all too aware of the three pairs of eyes watching them.

Seemingly oblivious to the tension between Kane and Alex, Rocky launched into a gory description of a movie he and Heather had watched the week before, obviously thinking Kane would relish the hideous details as much as he did. Kane listened in silence for a moment, then glanced at Alex with an expressive grimace. "I think I'll have a chat with Polly about Heather's viewing habits."

"Good idea," Alex murmured. If she'd known Polly better, she probably would have done so herself.

Kane smoothly changed the subject, diverting Rocky's attention to his collection of Teenage Mutant Ninja Turtles. "Added any new ones since I saw them last?" he asked.

Rocky nodded eagerly and began to describe an assortment of characters that sounded only marginally better to Alex than the *Terminator*. Still, Kane seemed more relaxed about the new topic, so Alex assumed TMNTs were more acceptable for a rather bizarre five-year-old. Were all little boys so ghoulish? Not having any personal experience with them, Alex couldn't say.

And to think how many times during the past few years she'd thought wistfully of having children. After this afternoon with the Simpson children, she realized that child-raising wasn't exactly as sweet and simple as it had seemed in her vague biological-clock-inspired daydreams. Maybe she wasn't cut out for that responsibility.

She glanced up from her half-eaten cookie to find herself the recipient of a broad, dimpled smile from Casey. "Good cookies, Alex," the child said, as though sensing Alex needed a word of encouragement.

Alex returned the smile. "I'm glad you're enjoying them, Casey." Maybe she'd get the hang of this, after all, with a little more practice.

After snack time, Kane dug out a children's book from his mother's bookshelves, then held Kelly on his knee while Alex held Casey and read the story aloud, using every funny voice she could summon to keep the children entertained. It wasn't easy to concentrate on the story, when Kane continued to look at her, as though he was still hungry and she was an even more delectable snack than his mother's homemade cookies. Nor was she able to ignore how very appealing Kane looked with a toddler cuddled on his lap.

Read the story, Alexandra, before you make an utter fool of yourself.

She managed, somehow. Even Rocky deigned to listen, lying on his stomach on the floor and kicking his sneakered feet behind him, when he finally forgot to be cool and started laughing, along with the twins.

Dottie found them, just that way, when she walked into the den with Mildred and Polly, the children's mother, at her heels. "Well, isn't this nice," Dottie said, giving Alex a brilliant smile.

Rocky looked up at his mother. "Did the dentist make your mouth bleed, Mom? Did he use the drill? Was it gross?"

Polly sighed. "Honestly, Rocky. Where do you get those ideas?"

Alex and Kane shared a laughing glance over the heads of the twins.

Dottie watched them with a contented smile.

10

ALEX AND KANE didn't have a chance to speak in private for some time after Polly left with her children. Dottie and Mildred explained that the bazaar committee would be coming by later for a last meeting prior to the event, but invited Kane to join them for a light dinner, an invitation he accepted. Dottie and Mildred headed for the kitchen to warm the food they'd prepared earlier and assemble the sweets they intended to serve to the committee, leaving Alex and Kane alone in the den.

Kane had just started to speak when Johnnie Mae arrived home from her customer greeter's job and proceeded to tell him all about the exciting apprehension of a shoplifter that afternoon in the store where she worked. Snatching the momentary reprieve, Alex excused herself to freshen up. She took her time changing her clothing and repairing her hair and makeup, aware that Kane was waiting for her to return.

What would she say to him when he finally drew her away from the others? She knew he would do so. The intention had been quite clear in his expression before Johnnie Mae interrupted them. Would he demand an explanation for the way she'd run from his bedroom Sunday morning? For the way she'd avoided him since?

Or did he know, as she suspected he did, how deeply she'd been shaken by what had happened between them? How momentous that night had been for her?

How terribly she'd missed him during the hours they'd been apart since?

It would have been so easy to go to him during the two long, past nights. She'd been so tempted to cross the lawns and throw herself into the arms she knew would be waiting to welcome her. But she'd made herself stay away, made herself think of all the reasons why she didn't want to get involved with him.

She had a life in Chicago, an apartment, friends, commitments. As much as she'd enjoyed her time in Andersenville, she'd never given serious consideration to moving to a small, Southern town, having always thrived on the fast pace of the city. And she'd spent so much of her childhood trying to entertain herself alone, while longing for her parents to return from their demanding, almost all-consuming jobs. Did she really want to spend the rest of her life doing the same with Kane?

She'd told herself repeatedly that things were different now. She was no longer a child, but a strong, self-sufficient, independent adult. She had a career of her own; she *needed* time alone to do her own work! She'd also been telling herself, for the past five years, that she wanted a family, so she wouldn't feel so totally alone.

But old resentments, old feelings of neglect, old insecurities had a nasty way of hanging around, long after childhood had passed, and Alex knew very well she hadn't completely recovered from hers. What if that old baggage came between Kane and herself? What if her insecurity made it impossible for her ever to accept his other responsibilities, so that they only ended up hurting each other, no matter how badly they wanted each other now?

And what if he discovered that he wanted a more traditional woman, after all, one raised in the same town, with the same customs, the same background? A woman less likely to remind him of the one who'd once hurt him so badly?

Thoroughly frustrated, Alex brought down both fists upon the bathroom vanity, glaring fiercely into the mirror over the sink. "Dammit, Bennett, grow up!" she ordered herself between clenched teeth, furious at her uncharacteristic vacillating.

But sometimes it wasn't always easy to do what she should, even when she happened to know what that was. This time, she hadn't a clue.

By the time Alex rejoined the others, Dottie and Mildred had removed the pot roast from the slow cooker in which it had been cooking all day, heated the vegetables they'd prepared to go with it, taken the rolls out of the oven and were ready to serve dinner. The ladies kept up a lively conversation during the meal, giving Kane and Alex little opportunity to do more than slip in an occasional comment or question.

Alex frequently felt Kane's eyes on her during the meal. Their gazes met more than once, and when they did, Alex wondered if her intimate memories were as apparent to Kane as his were to her.

The dinner dishes had barely been cleared away when the first of the committee members arrived, Pearl and Melanie, as it happened. Melanie greeted Alex warmly, then acknowledged Kane with a friendly smile.

"Anything juicy you want to tell me?" she asked Alex in a murmur, when the others were otherwise occupied.

"Like what?" Alex whispered, wondering if Melanie already knew her well enough to tell that something momentous had happened since the last time they'd been together.

Melanie's eyebrows lifted at something she must have seen in Alex's expression. "It was only a passing question, but now I'm wondering if you *do* have something to tell me."

But Alex wasn't quite ready to talk about her relationship with Kane—if it could be called that. For one thing, she was well aware that Melanie was still a contender for Kane's attentions—to Mildred, if to no one else.

Their murmured conversation was interrupted when more committee members arrived, chattering and laughing, gravitating to the snacks Dottie, Mildred and Johnnie Mae had set out in the dining room. Most of the guests were drinking coffee from the silver service on the buffet, but Dottie had also prepared a fruit punch, which she served in a sparkling, antique glass punch bowl.

As Melanie's attention was claimed by someone else, Alex heard Dottie give an annoyed exclamation. "Oh, dear. I forgot to bring in the extra bag of ice from the storage room freezer."

Since Dottie had her hands full, Alex was just about to volunteer to fetch the ice, when an auburn-haired woman in a bright green dress offered instead. "I'll get it, Dottie. It's the least I can do, since you wouldn't allow me to provide any snacks for this evening."

"Oh, Mildred and I didn't mind taking care of the snacks, Ethel. But I would appreciate your getting the ice for me. You know where the freezer is, don't you?"

"Heavens, yes. I've only been coming to this house for the past thirty years or so, Dottie Lovell!"

Dottie laughed brightly and turned back to her hostessing, just as Alex was distracted by Kane, who'd walked up behind her after Melanie stepped away. "How about if we cut out of here when the committee meeting begins?" Kane asked in a low voice meant just for her.

"We could go for a drive," he added when she looked at him questioningly. "It's a nice evening for one."

She knew she'd stalled as long as she could—as long as she wanted to, for that matter. It was time she and Kane talked. She only wished she knew what she was going to say to him. "All right. That sounds nice."

He gave her a smile of approval. "You know, of course, that we'll set all the tongues wagging for the remainder of the committee meeting."

Alex grimaced. "I really needed to hear that."

He chuckled and brushed her cheek with the back of his knuckles. "Too late to back out now, honey."

Though the drawled endearment made a ripple of pleasure course down her spine, the pleasure was tempered by her worry that his words might be more prophetic than even he knew.

And then a bloodcurdling scream from the direction of the kitchen ripped through the room, instantly silencing the babble of conversation and laughter. For just a moment everyone froze, uncertain what had happened. The scream was followed by a distinct thud.

"Oh, no! *Cujo!*" Dottie cried, clapping her hands over her mouth.

Having been closest to the kitchen door, Kane and Alex were already dashing that way. Remembering that Ethel had been on her way to the freezer, in the storage room on the other side of the kitchen, Alex groaned, suddenly realizing along with Dottie what must have happened.

Sure enough, they found poor Ethel flat on her back on the storage room floor, surrounded by ice cubes and a flat board, on which sat a very large, very hairy and very frozen corpse. Alex shuddered, knowing how she would have reacted if she'd reached into someone's freezer and pulled out a tarantula. She'd have been on the floor, just like Ethel.

Muttering a curse beneath his breath, Kane knelt to one side of the shaken woman. Alex shoved the board out of her way, careful not to touch the thing pinned to it, and knelt at Ethel's other side. Dottie, Mildred, Johnnie Mae and several others crowded into the doorway, Johnnie Mae wringing her hands, Mildred scolding, Dottie jabbering apologies. The noise was deafening.

Kane held up a hand. "Quiet, please," he said, without raising his voice.

Alex's eyes widened when the group immediately fell silent. Kane could be a handy sort of guy to have around, she found herself thinking inconsequentially.

"Ethel?" Kane asked gently. "Are you all right?"

Ethel looked very embarrassed, though her hands were still trembling visibly. "Oh, yes, I'm fine. It's just that I hadn't expected—"

"It belongs to my nephew, Jason," Johnnie Mae burst out in distress. "I killed it with poisoned crickets, and I wanted to save it for him so he could have it mounted if he wanted to. . . . Of course, I didn't mean to kill it, but—"

"I just knew something like this would happen," Mildred cut in curtly. "It's bad enough that we've had to live with that thing in there. Lord knows, I tried to get you to throw it out. But now you've terrorized one of our guests. If you'd only listen to me once in a while, maybe—"

"It's my fault!" Dottie wailed, her hands on her cheeks as she gazed apologetically at Ethel. "I forgot all about it being in there. Oh, Ethel, can you ever forgive me?"

But Ethel was already rising to her feet, with Kane and Alex's assistance, shaking her head firmly. "Now, Dottie, don't make a fuss. It just gave me a start, that's all. And Johnnie Mae, you know I raised five boys of my own. You wouldn't believe some of the things that ended up in my freezer during the years. Not to mention under my bed."

"I only hope Jason is as understanding as you are, when he gets home next week and finds out I've murdered his pet," Johnnie Mae said with a deep sigh.

"You haven't told him yet?" Mildred demanded. "Johnnie Mae, that boy's called here twice, asking about that creature!"

"I know." Johnnie Mae shuffled her feet, the picture of guilt. "I didn't have the heart to ruin his trip by breaking the news to him."

"Well, what did you tell him?"

"I just assured him that Cujo was still in one piece," Johnnie Mae admitted. "Well, it was the truth! I just didn't mention that it was dead."

"Honest to goodness, Johnnie Mae, you haven't got the sense God gave a goose. Of all the harebrained . . ."

"Now don't you two start," Dottie warned sharply. "We have guests. Ethel, would you like to lie down for a moment?"

"Of course I don't want to lie down! I'm chairman of this committee, and it's time we start our meeting. We've got a dozen things to decide tonight if we're going to have a bazaar next weekend."

Kane touched Alex's shoulder. "This is our chance," he murmured.

"Kane, are you leaving?" Dottie asked. The others turned back toward the dining room, nervous laughter breaking out among them as they verbally replayed Ethel's scene.

"Alex and I are going to take a drive, maybe get some ice cream or something," Kane explained, already inching toward the back door. "We don't want to interfere with your meeting."

Dottie nodded approval. "Good idea. This is probably going to be a very dull meeting, now that the real excitement is over. You kids have fun."

Feeling like a teenager leaving with her high school boyfriend, Alex slipped into a lightweight jacket and escaped the house with Kane. It was only a little after seven. At least, she thought with an attempt at humor, Dottie hadn't given them a ten o'clock curfew! They could probably stay out until . . . oh, ten-thirty before the real gossip began!

They said very little as Kane pulled out of his driveway. He drove seemingly aimlessly for a while, soft music from the radio providing the only sound in the car. And then he made a turn that brought them onto a narrow, secluded lane Alex recognized instantly. It was the path to the small pond where they'd parked, the night he'd driven her home from the church social. She supposed that was as good a place as any to talk in private.

She clenched her hands in her lap, nervously wondering what she was going to say to him. What he expected her to say.

Kane parked his car in a small clearing beside the pond, giving them a clear view of the romantically moon-silvered water. He stared straight ahead through the windshield, clearing his throat as if about to speak, then falling silent again as though he couldn't think of anything to say. Alex glanced sideways at him through her lashes, at the same time he turned to look at her.

"That was some excitement back at Mother's, wasn't it?" he asked, obviously deciding to start the conversation casually.

"Mmm . . . yes, it was. Ethel has a rather dramatic scream, doesn't she?"

Alex bit her lip, trying not to giggle at the memory. She'd really felt quite sorry for Ethel. She shouldn't . . . And then her gaze clashed with Kane's through the shadows in the car.

They started laughing at exactly the same moment.

"Oh, we shouldn't," Alex protested through her laughter, her hands pressed to her cheeks. "It really wasn't funny. But, oh, Kane . . ."

"I know," he said with a grin. "The thought of Ethel reaching into that freezer and pulling out that—"

"Don't," Alex begged, giggling helplessly, even as she shuddered in sympathy with Dottie's unfortunate friend. "I can't even think about it."

"Yeah. Poor Ethel. She must have thought it was long past time someone around there cleaned out the freezer. I mean, I've grown some fuzzy green things in leftover dishes before, but Cujo's got me beat."

"Can you imagine how Jason's going to react, when he stops to pick up his pet and finds him frozen on a board?"

"I'll have to remember never to ask Johnnie Mae to watch my dog, if I ever get around to buying one."

Alex laughed. "Poor Johnnie Mae. I'm sure she means well. She's just a little . . ."

"Odd. Always has been. She drives Aunt Mildred nuts."

"Still, they seem to be good friends," Alex mused, thinking of the unusual relationship between the women.

"Yeah. I think both of them enjoy their bickering. If they didn't, they'd never have been able to live in the same house this long."

Alex rested her head against the back of her seat and looked out over the little pond. "It's so peaceful here."

"Hmm. I used to fish here when I was a kid. Even cut school a time or two, to spend the afternoon with a fishing pole and a bucket of worms. Right over there, underneath that big willow," he added, pointing out the spot.

Picturing a young, shirtless, barefoot Kane, enjoying a quiet afternoon on his own, Alex smiled. "I'm sure Dottie didn't approve of your cutting school."

"Hardly. I was grounded for a month the last time I did it. It was worth it, though," Kane added reflectively. "Caught the biggest crappie I ever hooked that afternoon. Mom fried it up for me that night, even though she was mad as a wet hen that I'd left school."

"You're very fortunate to have such an understanding mother."

"What were you like as a girl, Alex?" Kane asked unexpectedly.

She shrugged. "Quiet. Studious. Always in my room with my books and the stories I was writing, even then."

He reached out to thread his fingers through her curls. "Do you realize that we almost didn't meet at all? If you hadn't got lost . . ."

"If that cow hadn't run me off the road . . ."

"I'm sorry you hurt your head and wrecked your car," Kane murmured, lifting his other hand to cup her face "but I'm very glad you wandered into my town, Alexandra Bennett."

He lowered his mouth to hers before she could tell him that she was also glad fate had brought her into his path. Whatever happened between them, she'd hate to think she'd have gone through the rest of her life without ever having known Dr. Kane Lovell.

Alex watched Kane through her lashes as he nibbled at her mouth, tugging her lower lip between his teeth, soothing it with his tongue, taking his time to thoroughly explore every inch of her mouth before kissing her more deeply, more hungrily. Alex slid her fingers into his hair and held him tightly to her, returning the kiss just as eagerly.

"Alex," Kane groaned into her mouth. "I've wanted you so badly the past two days. I've tried to give you time, but . . ." He kissed her again.

"I know, Kane." Her words came out in a husky whisper. "I've missed you, too. It's just that I was—" Her voice trailed away.

He pressed his lips to her throat encouragingly. "What, honey?"

"Scared," she admitted, hiding her face in his shoulder.

"I know," he murmured, his hand warm on her back. "Me, too."

That startled her into lifting her head. "You? Why?"

"Because I can't bear the thought of your leaving, now that we've been together. I hate the thought of you going back to that other man," he said roughly. "Dammit, Alex, you're in my blood now. I've held you, touched you, tasted you. I've watched you come apart in my arms. Do you really think I can stand aside and watch you walk away from me now?"

"Kane, I—"

His hand tightened convulsively in her hair. "I want you. I've never wanted anyone like this. And you want me, too, Alex. Dammit, I know you do. I've seen it in your eyes."

"Yes," she whispered, unable to deny what both of them knew. "I want you, Kane. But—"

"Then don't fight me, honey. Give me a chance. Give *us* a chance," he murmured, his lips hovering inches above her own. "Let me show you how good we can be together."

She already knew how good they could be together—at least in one way. Whatever other obstacles lay between them, they were very well matched physically. She responded to him as she had to no one else, ached for him as she'd never imagined wanting anyone before.

If only she could believe that what they had was more than physical, more than temporary, more than a potentially devastating error of judgment. If only she could trust her own tangled emotions, as well as his.

"Kane, I don't—"

But again he gave her no chance to finish the sentence. His mouth abruptly covered hers smothering the words, as though he refused to hear them. As though he'd known he wouldn't like what she had intended to say.

As though he realized that he had more effective inducements than mere words.

She could have withstood the words—perhaps. Could have countered his persuasion—maybe. But she couldn't resist his desire, couldn't hold back, when he kissed her as though she was the only woman in the world for him. As though he really had never wanted anyone more.

How could she resist what she'd always hoped to find in a man's arms?

Her arms tightened around his neck. Her lips parted. Kane groaned deep in his chest and thrust his tongue into her mouth, fitting them more tightly together. His hands swept her body, feverishly, demandingly, stoking fires wherever they touched, coaxing responses she couldn't have held back, had she tried. She shuddered beneath the onslaught, felt her legs parting when his hand fell to her thigh, slipping beneath her full skirt.

"Kane," she whispered, her head falling back when he released her mouth to lower his lips to her throat. "Oh, Kane."

He answered the unspoken plea by unbuttoning her blouse. A moment later she sighed in mingled relief and delight when his warm mouth settled hungrily on the hardened tip of one aching, desire-swollen breast. At the same time, his hand moved skillfully between her legs and she shivered, her fingers tightening in his thick, dark hair. "Kane!"

He shifted to draw her closer, then cursed the low console between them. "Dammit, Alex, I'm too old to make love in a car," he muttered with a rough mixture of frustration and amusement. "Let me take you home, sweetheart."

Her smile felt wicked, even to her. She drew one hand slowly down his chest. "Oh, I don't know," she murmured seductively, tugging lightly at his nipples through his shirt and smiling more deeply when he groaned in response. "I've never made love in a car. I was always such a properly behaved young woman. Don't you think you could remember how, if you really put your mind to it?"

Kane gave a gravelly chuckle and moved his thumb in a slow circle, making Alex gasp and arch upward on the seat. "I'm sure we could work something out," he said. "But we'd be so much more comfortable in my big, warm bed. Naked."

"Hmm." She pretended to consider his words, dropping her hand to stroke his firm thigh from the knee upward. "That does sound tempting," she conceded, moving her fingers slowly inward, just brushing the length of him through the straining fabric of his slacks. "But . . ."

And then her seeking fingers connected with something hard and unyielding. And it wasn't Kane.

This time his pager didn't have to make a sound to ruin her evening. Alex closed her eyes, her mood swiftly changing from playfully sensual to bleakly sober. She was beginning to believe Kane's pager was a symbol of everything that stood between them, every reservation she had about their relationship. It always seemed to show up at the most significant times.

Kane realized that something had changed, drastically. "Alex? What is it? What's wrong?"

She drew herself slowly out of his arms. "I think we'd better go back now. It's getting late."

"We've only been gone a little over an hour. What—?" His hand covered hers at his waist, then went still. "Oh."

She pulled away, clasping her hands together in her lap, the feel of the pager still imprinted on her fingers. "I wonder if the committee meeting is over yet."

"Alex, I have to wear the pager. Even when I'm not on call, I don't like to be out of reach, if one of my patients needs me."

She turned her head to look out the window at her side, staring blindly at the woods beyond the pond. "I know, Kane."

"Even if I were called away, it wouldn't mean you were any less important to me," he persisted. "I'm not sure you realize exactly how important you are to me. But that doesn't mean I can forget about the others who need me. There are so few doctors in this area, so many people who can't afford—or who don't have the time— to drive to one of the larger cities for medical treatment. In an emergency, I have to be available."

"I know that, Kane. Really. I understand."

"But you resent it," he said, his tone grim.

"No," she whispered, still looking away from him. "I admire you for your dedication, for your willingness to put your own life aside for the people who need you, who depend on you. Who've put their very lives in your hands. You're a very special man, Kane. I just don't know if I can be as patient and unselfish as you are."

"Alex. Please. Come home with me. Let's talk about this some more."

"No. Not tonight. When I'm alone with you, I—I can't think. I can't be logical and rational and careful. I want you so much that all I can think of is being close to you. But I'm afraid that if I let myself get too deeply involved now, before I know I can handle it, I'll only end up hurting us both. And I couldn't bear to hurt you, Kane."

"Dammit, Alex. You're giving up on us, without even giving us a chance. I know my work is demanding, that my loyalties are somewhat divided. But that doesn't mean I can't have a life of my own, as well. That I can't fall in love, have a family, have the things that other men have. Does it?"

"No," she murmured, blinking back tears. "You can have all that, Kane. You deserve it all. I just don't know if I'm the one to help you achieve those things. I don't know if I can."

"Or if you want to? Would you be happier if I moved to Chicago and took on a nice, undemanding, eight to five, dermatology practice?" he asked bitterly. "Hell, I could even join a country club and take up golf. I understand it's the game of all the high-society doctors."

She turned then, so rapidly that her hair whipped around her face. "Don't you *dare* compare me to Cathy! I've never asked you to give up anything. You belong here, Kane. These people need you. And you need them. Don't you think I know that?"

"They're fine people, Alex. It's a good life here."

"Yes," she agreed. "I know it is. I just don't know if it's right for me."

He sighed and ran a hand through his hair. "You've only been here a couple of weeks. Maybe you just need more time."

She swallowed. "I think what I really need is to go home."

He grew still. "I hope you mean my mother's house."

"No. I mean *my* home. Chicago."

Kane gripped the steering wheel so tightly, she could see his knuckles gleaming in the shadows. She knew he was having to make an effort to keep from reaching out to her. "When?" he asked curtly.

"Soon. I've done all the research I need for my book. I'm ready to start writing."

"You can write here."

"I could, yes. But I need to go home. I need to think, Kane. I can't do that here, surrounded by you and your mother and her friends. I've had a wonderful time in Andersenville, I really have. I just don't know if I'm ready to walk away from everything I have in Chicago, just because I've had two lovely weeks here."

"Is that all I've been to you?" He spoke softly, so softly she almost had to strain to hear him. "A lovely, two-week vacation fling?"

She closed her eyes against the sound of pain in his voice. "I don't know what you want from me," she whispered. "I don't know what you want me to say."

He was silent for what seemed like a very long time. When he finally spoke again, his voice had changed, become rougher, harder. "If you don't even know what I want, then maybe you *should* go home. Maybe you do need time. Time to realize what I'm offering. And time to decide whether I'm offering enough for you."

She didn't know what to say. She wanted so badly to tell him that whatever he offered would be enough, that she wanted him badly enough to accept whatever he had to give. But something held the words inside her. Maybe the old fears and insecurities left over from her childhood. Or maybe a whole new set of fears and insecurities directly related to Kane. Whatever the reason, she remained silent, staring fiercely at her hands.

After another long, tense moment, Kane exhaled sharply and started the engine. He didn't speak as he threw the car into reverse and turned onto the lane leading away from the pond. Alex allowed herself only one wistful glance over her shoulder. How quickly humor and desire had turned to despair!

11

SEVERAL CARS were just pulling out of Dottie's driveway, so Alex assumed the committee meeting had ended. Identifying the only remaining vehicle as Melanie's, she swallowed a sigh, knowing the other woman would be curious as to why she and Kane had returned so early, what had gone on between them. And Dottie, of course, was probably just as curious, if not more.

That was just one more drawback to conducting a romance, however ill-fated, with a man as visible as Kane. There was little privacy allowed to them.

"Are you coming in?" she asked, speaking for the first time since they'd left the pond.

Kane hesitated, then shook his head. "No. Tell Mother I'll see her tomorrow, okay?"

Another potential problem, Alex thought, pulling her sweater more snugly around her. Kane was devoted to his mother and would always make her an important part of his life, particularly since she lived right next door and probably would, for as long as she was able to live on her own. Some women might have problems dealing with having a man's mother become such a major part of their relationship.

Of course, if Alex were to have a mother-in-law in her life, she couldn't imagine a nicer one than Dottie Lovell, she thought with a touch of wistfulness. "I'll tell her."

Kane flexed his hands on the steering wheel. "When are you leaving?"

She swallowed hard. "I may as well leave tomorrow. There's really no reason for me to stay any longer."

He grimaced. "Will you answer one question for me?"

She eyed him warily. "If I can."

"Do you love him?"

Had she been asked the same question two weeks ago, she might have had more difficulty answering. Now she didn't even hesitate. "No."

"Then why are you going back to him?"

"I'm not going back to Bill," she replied quietly. "Whatever else happens, I won't be seeing him anymore. It wouldn't be fair to him."

"Then stay here," he said, turning to cradle her cheek in one large, strong hand. "I won't rush you. I'll give you all the time and space you need. Just don't go back to Chicago, Alex. Not now."

Was he really so afraid she'd forget him, forget everything between them, if she went back to Chicago? And didn't he realize that she had to find out if he was right? That she had to know there was more between them than physical infatuation, or being thrown together by circumstances? That too much was at stake to make decisions influenced by fiery emotions and volatile passion?

"I need that time, Kane," she whispered, nestling her face into his palm for one, stolen moment. "And I need to go home. I have to be sure."

"I told myself I wouldn't stand by and watch you walk out of my life," he growled. "That I'd fight to keep you here if I had to. But I can't hold you, if you don't want to stay."

His voice hardened. "Run home to Chicago, Alex. Try to forget me, if you can. Tell yourself it was only a vacation fling or a fleeting infatuation. But when you think about me, think about the way you feel when we're together, the way you felt in my arms, in my bed. Ask yourself if anyone else will ever make you feel this way—and if you can live the rest of your life, never knowing these feelings again."

He brought his mouth down upon hers almost before he finished speaking, giving her no chance to respond, even had she known what to say in return. His tongue stabbed into her mouth, deepening the kiss, and he pulled her closer, so that the only thing separating them was the low console between their straining bodies.

The kiss lasted a very long time. By the time Kane released her, Alex was almost ready to promise him anything he wanted. She burned for him, ached for him, wanted nothing more than to throw herself upon him and beg him to carry her to his house and make love to her for the rest of her life. Yet some tiny remnant of fear lingered within her, giving her the strength to pull out of his arms and wrench open her door.

She slipped from the car and all but ran up the walk to the front porch. Kane didn't try to stop her.

ALEX WOULD HAVE GIVEN almost anything to have been able to slip into the house without anyone seeing her, without having to face Kane's mother or her friends. But she knew it couldn't be that easy. Calling on every ounce of poise she'd developed over the years, she shuttered her expression, locked her distress deeply inside her, and managed a smile as she entered the den, where it appeared that Melanie and Pearl were just taking their leave of the others.

"Why, Alex. You're home early," Dottie said, looking just a bit disappointed. "Did Kane have another emergency?"

"No. I have a few things to do tonight, and Kane went on home to get some rest. He asked me to tell you he'd talk to you tomorrow," Alex explained, sliding her hands into the deep, side pockets of her sweater. She took a deep breath to prepare herself for the announcement she had to make.

She couldn't think of any way to begin, except to just get it out. "I'll be going back to Chicago tomorrow. I'll probably leave before noon."

Dottie made a sound of protest, her eyes widening. "Going back? Oh, Alex, must you?"

"You're leaving so soon?" Johnnie Mae asked, characteristically wringing her pudgy hands. "Oh, we've so enjoyed having you here."

"I've enjoyed being here," Alex replied gently. "But I've finished my research. I have to get back to work."

"I'll miss you, Alex," Melanie said softly, her smile looking a bit sad. "I've so enjoyed knowing you."

Alex forced a smile in return. "It's not as though we're saying goodbye forever. We'll stay in touch, okay?"

"Sure. We'll do that," Melanie agreed, though she sounded doubtful. She probably knew, as Alex did, that long-distance friendships were difficult to maintain, particularly when they were as new as theirs.

Melanie and Pearl didn't linger after that. With final farewells to Alex, they left.

"I think I'll say good-night now," Alex told the others, unable to sustain her casual facade any longer. "I have a few calls to make and some packing to do."

"We'll have a nice breakfast together before you leave," Johnnie Mae offered.

Alex nodded. "I'd like that. Good night."

She was aware that Dottie watched her sadly as she left the room.

Finally alone, Alex sat on the edge of her bed and buried her face in her hands, allowing her shoulders to slump, her eyes to mist. Leaving Kane's arms had been the hardest thing she'd ever done. She tried to tell herself it might have also been the wisest. If it hurt this badly now, how much worse would it have been, if they'd spent even more time together?

"YOU REALLY HAVE TO go now, Alex?" Dottie asked again the next morning, as Alex prepared to carry the last of her things to the rented car she would drive back to Chicago. "Can't you stay a little longer?"

Alex shook her head. "I'm afraid not, Dottie. I'd love to, but I have obligations in Chicago that I must get back to. I hope you understand."

Dottie nodded reluctantly. "I'll miss you."

Alex felt her smile waver. "I'll miss you, too. You've been wonderful to me. I don't know what I would have done, if you hadn't been here after my accident."

"You drive carefully this time, you hear?" Johnnie Mae admonished Alex, hovering nearby.

"I will," Alex promised. "I'll watch for cows," she added, making an attempt at humor to lighten the gravity of their parting.

"You have all your things? You haven't forgotten anything?" Mildred, ever the practical one, inquired.

"No, I'm not leaving anything," Alex answered. *Nothing except my heart, that is.*

"I wish Kane hadn't had to leave for the hospital so early this morning," Dottie fretted. "I'm sure he would have liked to see you off."

Alex only smiled, well aware that Kane's early departure had been no coincidence. He'd probably been as anxious as Alex to avoid a prolonged, goodbye scene.

"I'd better be going," she said, taking one last glance around the home where she'd been welcomed so warmly, so generously. "I'll call when I get home," she added, reaffirming a promise she'd made earlier to ease Dottie's concern about her traveling alone.

"You do that," Dottie said, holding out her arms. "Drive carefully, Alex."

Alex hugged Dottie warmly, blinking back tears. "I will. Bye, Dottie."

And then she turned to hug Johnnie Mae, who returned the embrace with enough enthusiasm to almost take Alex's breath away. Only then did Alex turn more cautiously to Mildred, uncertain how to take her leave of Dottie's stern, though endearing sister. She was startled to see that Mildred's gray eyes were damp.

"We've enjoyed having you here, Alex," Mildred said, holding herself as straight as ever. "You take care of yourself."

"You, too," Alex whispered, kissing the older woman's lined cheek. "Bye, Mildred."

She managed not to let the tears fall until she was in her car, driving away from the old Victorian house that had looked so daunting during that thunderstorm and appeared so very different now. Dashing at her wet cheeks with the back of one hand, she told herself that it wasn't forever, that she'd see Dottie and the others again. That she'd see Kane again. But still the tears fell, dripping steadily down her chin.

She thought she caught a glimpse of black and white out of the corner of her eye, just as she left the town of Andersenville behind her. She turned her head quickly, half expecting to see the cow that had stranded her here, in the first place. But it was a figment of her imagination, she decided, when she saw nothing but woods and fields.

Maybe it had all been nothing more than imagination—a fleeting fantasy, destined to conclude with the return of reality.

But, oh, how it hurt to see the fantasy end!

"WELL, I GUESS that answers your question, Dottie," Mildred said flatly as the three women watched Alex's car disappear down the road. "Alex wasn't the right one for Kane."

Dottie wiped delicately at one corner of her eye with the corner of the apron she'd worn to prepare breakfast. "I was so sure she was the one. He was so taken with her."

"And she passed every test the two of you schemed up for her," Johnnie Mae agreed wistfully. "Not always the way you expected her to, but always cleverly."

Mildred shook her head, looking almost as regretful as the other two. "Looks like she failed the most important test of all."

"What's that?"

"She left."

The three women remained where they were for several more minutes, staring thoughtfully at the spot where they'd last seen Alex. How would Kane feel when he came home, to find her gone?

SOMEHOW KANE KNEW she was gone, the moment he pulled into his driveway and glanced across the lawn toward his mother's house. The room in which Alex had slept was dark. Even the windows looked empty, though the white lace curtains Dottie had hung a few months ago still fluttered there.

She was gone. And Kane felt as empty inside as the room in which Alex had stayed so briefly.

ALEX HAD NEVER MINDED living alone. She'd been comfortable with her own company for most of her life. She'd learned, as a solitary child, to keep herself entertained with her books and writing and a radio for background noise. She'd never really been lonely before.

She was lonely now.

It was Sunday, over a month since her return from Andersenville, and she still couldn't get her two-week idyll out of her mind, no matter how desperately she pursued her former activities. She'd spent time with friends, busied herself with the new book—her editor had already enthusiastically approved a preliminary synopsis—immersed herself in further research. She'd even gone on an uncharacteristic cleaning spree until her apartment looked like a television ad for Mr. Clean. And still she couldn't forget.

So many times she'd thought of picking up the phone. Calling Dottie or Melanie.

Calling Kane.

Her hand had actually fallen upon the receiver a time or two, before she'd allowed her fears to stop her yet again. At first, she'd worried whether she was willing to make the compromises necessary for involvement with Kane Lovell.

As the weeks passed with no word from him, her doubts changed. What if he'd realized that her leaving had been the best thing for him? What if he'd decided she wasn't right for him, after all, that he'd been under the influence of a passing, albeit powerful, attraction when he'd made his rash requests and promises?

What if he'd taken a good look around him and realized that Alex didn't really belong in his world, that there were other women who fitted into his life much more smoothly, much more naturally? Melanie, for example.

It had been five weeks since Alex had left. Had Kane looked to Melanie for companionship during that time? Had he consoled himself with her warm smile and gentle humor, her gourmet cooking and intelligent conversation?

Had he forgotten all about Alex, even though she'd been dismally unable to put him out of her mind? Out of her heart?

She'd spent many long, lonely nights, remembering the one night in his arms, regretting that there hadn't been more. Wondering if she'd ever feel like that again. Knowing she wouldn't, not with anyone but Kane.

She was an emotional wreck. And damned if she knew what she was going to do about it.

KANE RESTLESSLY PACED his den in the middle of another long, lonely night. He couldn't sleep, wasn't interested in anything on television. Since Alex had left, he'd already read all her books, twice, but they only made him ache all the harder for the bright, funny, perceptive and imaginative woman who'd written them. For once, he would have almost welcomed the sound of his pager. Not that he really wanted a medical emergency, of course. It was just that he would have welcomed a distraction from his thoughts.

He missed her. She'd spent only two weeks with him, and yet he missed her more than he'd ever missed anyone, longed for her with an intensity that left him bruised and aching.

It hadn't been a passing attraction. Hadn't been the painful, youthful infatuation he'd felt for Cathy. This time it had been the real thing. Permanent.

He glanced across the room and down the hallway, where his empty bed awaited him. And, though he desperately needed the rest, he couldn't make himself walk down that hall, knowing that memories of Alex waited there to haunt him.

Needing to fill the taunting silence in his house, he abruptly snapped on the stereo in the built-in entertainment center on one wall of the large room. And winced when Hal Ketchum's smooth voice mourned his lost love, wondering if he was past the point of rescue from his pain. He'd sworn he'd never love that way again, the singer asserted. Yet here he was, brought to his knees again.

Kane groaned and turned the radio off.

He hadn't come to his knees yet. But he was close. Damned close.

Maybe it was time he did something about it.

IT WAS LATE on another Sunday afternoon when Alex found herself standing in front of the telephone, yet again. She hadn't consciously approached it this time, couldn't even remember getting up from the couch, where she'd been trying to read the newspaper.

"Dammit, Bennett, you're losing your mind," she scolded herself aloud, just to hear a voice in the silence. "You've got to snap out of this!"

But still the telephone held her gaze, drawing her like a magnet. Her hand almost tingled with the need to reach out to it. Hesitantly, she closed her fingers around the receiver.

Okay, she decided. She'd do it. She'd call Dottie. Ask about everyone's health, inquire about the success of the long-planned, church bazaar Alex had so regretted missing. Perhaps casually ask about Kane.

Maybe she'd call Melanie. Melanie could catch Alex up on the local gossip. Could tell her if Kane had been coming around.

Or . . . she could call Kane. Just to make sure everyone was okay. Just to say hello. Just to burst into tears and tell him she'd missed him until she ached from it, and beg him to come take her away from all this.

And what if she called him, only to find out that he was no longer interested? Would he really have let her drive away so easily, if he'd truly wanted her to stay? It had been two months since she'd left Mississippi. Wouldn't he at least have called her once, if he'd really cared for her as much as he'd claimed?

"Damn," she whispered, letting her hand fall back to her side. "Oh, damn, Alex, what have you done?"

A persistent buzz from her intercom finally drew her attention away from the telephone.

Frowning, she wondered who was calling on her. She hadn't been expecting anyone, had few friends who were in the habit of dropping by without calling beforehand. She rarely received deliveries on Sundays, so it probably wasn't that.

She considered ignoring the summons. She wasn't at all sure she was in the mood to be sociable. She'd probably end up crying all over some poor acquaintance, who'd only stopped by for a cup of coffee and a few laughs.

Then again, maybe a cup of coffee and a few laughs were exactly what Alex needed this afternoon. Sighing, she reached abruptly for the intercom button. "Yes?"

"You want to let me in?"

She jerked her hand away from the button as though it had suddenly turned red-hot, then stood staring at it, openmouthed. A moment later an impatient buzz came again from the box on the wall. Alex's hand was shaking this time when she pressed the button. "*Kane?*"

"Yeah."

"What are you doing here?"

"Well, I didn't come all this way to stand in a corridor, talking to a box. Let me in, Alex." He sounded rather annoyed. She could almost believe he was as nervous as she suddenly was.

She took a deep, ragged breath and pressed the button to unlock the security door downstairs. Her hands were still shaking when she lifted them to smooth her hair. She scolded herself for acting like an adolescent, even as she checked her clothing and wished she was wearing something a bit more alluring than a black and turquoise running suit.

A firm rap on the door made her stomach do flip-flops. *Why was Kane here?*

She opened the door.

12

HE WORE a denim jacket, a beige cotton sweater, faded jeans and scuffed, Western boots. His coffee-colored hair was tousled, his tanned face set in firm, serious lines. He looked more like a rancher than a physician. Alex had never seen anyone more beautiful in her life. "I can't believe you're here."

"Believe it," he advised, brushing past her when she didn't immediately invite him in. He glanced around her apartment, noting the eclectic decor, the expensive accoutrements.

"Nice place," he commented. "Shouldn't take you long to find another renter."

"A . . . er . . . another renter?" Alex repeated blankly.

He gave her an unsmiling look. "Yeah. When you leave."

"I'm leaving?"

"Damn straight, you are. Soon."

Alex resisted an impulse to shake her head in an attempt to clear it. Maybe she'd fallen asleep on the couch. Maybe this was only a dream. She gave Kane a suspicious frown. "Kane, *why* are you here?"

He smiled then, though faintly. "I'm here to carry you back to my kingdom, Alex. I hope you'll go willingly."

"Your kingdom?" she echoed, annoyed that she couldn't seem to stop parroting him.

His smile turned just a touch sheepish. "You're the one who compared small-town doctors to royalty."

The rest of what he'd said suddenly sank in. Her fingers clenched behind her. "You're here to take me back with you?"

"Over my shoulder, if necessary." He took two steps toward her, catching her forearms in firm, though gentle hands. "I've missed you, Alex. God, how I've missed you."

"Kane." She lifted her hands to his face, tentatively, almost afraid he'd vanish when she touched him. But he was warm and firm and oh, so real; she had never needed anything as much as she needed to feel his mouth on hers then. "Kiss me."

"Yes, ma'am," he murmured in his smooth, Mississippi drawl, sending ripples of pleasure all the way through her. His mouth covered hers and the ripples turned to shudders.

It was the most mind-shattering, life-altering kiss of Alex's experience. He didn't just kiss her, didn't just fuse his mouth with hers. He gave her his soul. And took hers in return.

It seemed like a very long time before Kane lifted his head. He touched her cheek, then glanced at his wet fingertips. Alex hadn't realized until then that she was crying.

Kane lifted his eyes back to hers, gave her a tender smile and kissed her again, so sweetly that her eyes flooded a second time.

But it wasn't long until sweetness changed to passion, until tenderness evaporated in the heat of building desire. Suddenly Kane was storming her mouth, his tongue surging between her parted lips, his hands sweeping her with growing demand. Already shaken by the beauty of those earlier kisses, Alex could only cling to him and lose herself in these new sensations, swept along by waves of hunger that seemed to course through both of them.

Cool air swept her skin when Kane tossed her running suit top aside. A moment later his hands warmed her, stroking her back, spanning her waist, kneading her breasts, sliding down her stomach to the elastic waistband of her slacks. And then he slipped one hand inside her slacks and panties, the tips of his fingers brushing the nest of curls between her legs.

Alex gasped into his mouth when his fingers slid lower, and her own hands tightened on his shoulders. She was trembling, aching, swollen and wet with wanting him, so ready for him that she thought she'd scream if she had to wait much longer. She tore at his clothing, shoving his jacket off his shoulders, pulling at the snap of his jeans. His impatience fueled by hers, Kane helped her, heedlessly tossing aside articles of clothing until they were both nude, straining together, groaning in unison at the pleasure of being so close, after being apart for so long.

Kane didn't even bother to try to find her bedroom. He lowered her to the carpet, right there in her living room, shoving aside one of his boots that lay in their way. Because they were both already thoroughly aroused, he made no further effort to prepare her and drove smoothly, powerfully, painlessly into her.

Alex gave a low moan of delight and wrapped her legs tightly around his lean hips as Kane surged into a steady rhythm that soon had her arching mindlessly, helplessly beneath him. She tried to say his name, but her voice was suddenly stolen from her in a rush of pleasure so intense that she gasped, then cried out, shuddering with the intensity of her climax. Kane was close behind her, grating her name between clenched teeth. He stiffened in her arms, surged deeper and faster into her, groaning at his release.

Long moments later, as Kane lay spent in her arms, his head cradled on her breast, while he fought to regain his breath, Alex realized she was crying again.

Incredible beauty always did that to her.

"WE NEED TO TALK," Kane said when both he and Alex had recovered from their lovemaking. He rose on one elbow and looked down at her, his mouth unsmiling, but his eyes so very tender.

She found herself trembling in reaction to his expression. No man had ever looked at her the way Kane was looking at her now. No man had ever seemed to want her this badly. But could he really love her enough to be sure they were right for each other? Sure enough that he'd come all the way to Chicago to take her back with him?

Over my shoulder, if necessary he'd said. Was he really prepared to go that far?

"Kane," she whispered through dry lips, "you hardly know me. We were together such a short time in Andersenville. There are so many things you don't know about me."

"What things?" he asked roughly. "Your favorite color? Your favorite song? Favorite foods? We have the rest of our lives to learn that sort of thing. I already know everything that matters."

She shook her head in disbelief. "Like what?"

"I know you're bright, talented, capable, resourceful. Sexy as hell. That you're kind, generous, thoughtful. I watched you with my mother and her friends, with fans of your writing, with Melanie, with Polly's children. You were wonderful with all of them. You're everything I've ever wanted, Alex. Everything I've ever hoped to find."

She swallowed a moan, desperately wanting to believe him. No one had ever described her so sweetly, so flatteringly. Her parents had loved her, but had wished she were more like them—brilliant, academic, less interested in worldly pursuits. Even Bill, who'd also claimed to love her, had often added that he only wished she were less obsessed with her work, more interested in sports, cooking, politics—the things he particularly enjoyed.

Kane hadn't tempered his praise with subtle criticism, as the others had. Which made his words so much harder to believe. Alex wasn't perfect, wasn't a paragon of any sort. If Kane truly thought she was, then it was even more of a mistake for them to get involved. She'd only end up disillusioning him, and would probably break her own heart, in the process.

"You haven't seen me at my worst," she murmured, ducking her head so she didn't have to see the emotions gleaming in his eyes. "I get too involved with my work much of the time, and I tend to neglect other people when I do. I forget appointments and obligations, and I get impatient and irritable, if I'm interrupted when

I'm really absorbed in my writing. I have a lot of insecurities, and I need a great deal of attention when I'm not obsessed with the writing. I'm an impulsive spender and I'm a terrible housekeeper and I never walk when I can drive, or cook when I can order out. I—"

Kane interrupted the ignominious list with a chuckle. "Are you trying to tell me that you have flaws, Alex? I never said I thought you were perfect. God knows, I'm not perfect, myself, so why would I want a perfect mate? I need someone warm and loving and kind and passionate. Someone who has her own life, her own interests, yet someone who still needs me as much as I need her. I need *you*, Alex. I love you."

Though she'd already seen the love in his eyes, it still shook her to hear the words. She hadn't quite realized how desperately she'd wanted, needed, to hear them.

"Oh, Kane," she whispered. "I don't know what to say."

"Say you love me," he suggested, reaching out to brush a strand of damp hair from her eyes. "I know you feel it, too, Alex. You couldn't make love with me like that and not feel it, too."

"I—" She swallowed hard, terrified. "I'm—"

"Afraid?"

She nodded miserably.

"Why, honey? Why did you run from me, when we both knew you wanted to stay?"

She didn't try to argue with him; she *had* wanted to stay. And she'd known it as well as he obviously did. "I was afraid it wasn't real," she muttered, darting a glance at him from beneath her lashes.

He looked only mildly amused. "Not real?"

He covered her left breast with his hand, both of them feeling the pulse pounding there. "Doesn't this feel real, sweetheart? Do I feel like an illusion to you?"

No, Kane was no illusion. And she was beginning to realize that her feelings for him were every bit as real.

Still, she tried to make him understand. "It happened so fast, so—so unbelievably. One moment I was lost on a highway in Mississippi, and the next I was stranded in a wonderful, friendly little town, surrounded by people who welcomed me as warmly as though they'd known me all my life. I was having a great time, was happier than I'd ever been, and yet it all seemed . . . surreal."

Kane chuckled, his fingers stroking her cheek, his eyes oddly understanding. "So you thought you'd stumbled upon Brigadoon, did you?"

She managed a weak smile. "Not Brigadoon, exactly. I just felt as though I'd wandered into a storybook town, where I didn't really belong. Especially after I met you."

She met his eyes squarely, aware that it was time to be totally, bravely honest. "I fell for you—so hard and so fast it terrified me. I couldn't believe you were really feeling the same things I was feeling. I couldn't believe it would last, once reality set in."

"It was always reality, Alex," Kane murmured. "It happened quickly, but I'd been looking for you for a very long time. I recognized you, almost the moment you came to me out of that storm. You were the woman I wanted to share my life, my home with. The only woman in the world who was everything I needed."

"Are you really sure, Kane?" she asked in a thin whisper, daring to hope that he was right. "Are you sure you wouldn't really like a different sort of woman—like Melanie, maybe?" she added in a rush.

He looked surprised. "Melanie?"

She nodded sheepishly. "She seemed so perfect for you. Beautiful, bright, raised in your town, patient with your schedule, so completely domestic. Your Aunt Mildred thought the two of you made the perfect couple."

"Melanie's a veritable paragon," Kane agreed gravely; his eyes glinted with amusement. "I'm sure she's practically perfect. I, however, don't happen to want a perfect paragon. I want you."

She couldn't help smiling. "Definitely not perfect."

"Perfect for me," he disputed, leaning over to kiss her firmly, though briefly.

Alex drew in a shaky breath, then released it in a rush of words. "I love you, Kane."

He grew still, hope flaring in his expression. "You're sure?"

"I have from the moment I saw you, I think."

A muscle jumped in his jaw; evidence of how tightly he was holding himself back. "I know it won't be easy," he seemed compelled to point out. "I'll try to clear more time for us. I've already hired a new, young doctor to replace Dr. Isaacs and relieve me of part of my caseload. He's covering for me now, as a matter of fact. Maybe we'll even be able to entice another doctor to join us, eventually, which will help even more.

"But, as much as I'd like to, I can't promise I won't ever be called away during important dinners, or miss family occasions, or forget to call when I'm detained by an emergency," he added candidly. "I can't promise to be there for you every time you want me, Alex, but I'll try my best to be there every time you need me."

Alex lifted a hand to his cheek, meeting his gaze with her own. "I can't promise that I won't sometimes resent your other obligations, that I won't sometimes feel neglected. But I'll always understand that you're doing what you have to do. What you were meant to do. Your dedication to your job, to your patients, to your family and your friends, is part of what makes you the very special man I love. How could I want you to be anything less?"

His eyes closed for a moment, then opened again, looking very bright. "I know you felt neglected by your parents," he murmured, covering her hand with his own. "I know they hurt you."

"Only because I was never entirely sure they really loved me," Alex admitted. "Because I never really believed I was more important to them than their work. As an adult, I can see that they did love me, that they tried their best to show me how they felt. They just didn't know how to express their feelings to a shy, insecure daydreamer of a child."

"That's one thing you'll never have to doubt," Kane told her without hesitation. "I intend to spend the rest of my life convincing you that I love you, that you're the most important person in my life, even when I can't always be with you. No one means more to me—no one, Alex. Not my patients, not my friends, my family—not even my mother, God help me. I love you. I need you to believe that."

She smiled mistily, wondering if teary eyes were going to become a chronic condition for her when she was with Kane. She'd never been one to cry easily before; but then, everything else had changed when she'd met this man. She'd probably better invest heavily in hankies. "I love you, Kane."

He smiled. "Good. Then maybe I won't have to carry you back to Mississippi on my shoulder, after all."

"No, that won't be necessary."

"When will you marry me? I'm warning you, I don't believe in long engagements."

"Long engagements?" she repeated with a skeptically lifted eyebrow. "Obviously, you don't even believe in long courtships. Kane, we only spent two weeks together—less than that, really, since we weren't together every day during that time."

He gave her a cocky grin. "As I said, when it's right, it's right. Time has nothing to do with it."

"And as I believe I mentioned before, you're an arrogant man, Kane Lovell."

"Mmm. But you love me, anyway?"

"I love you, anyway."

"And you'll marry me soon?"

"As soon as you want. When it's right, it's right."

He gave her a smacking kiss of approval. "Now you're talking."

She glanced down and heaved an exaggerated sigh. "I can't believe I just received and accepted a marriage proposal, lying nude on my living room floor."

Kane smiled. "Would you have preferred candles and flowers? A proposal on bended knee?"

"No. I wouldn't have changed a thing," she decided.

"Neither would I. As a matter of fact," he added, leaning over her, "there are certain parts I wouldn't mind doing again."

She trailed a finger down his chest. "What parts?"

"I'll show you," he promised. And did.

And again, she wouldn't have changed a thing.

Epilogue

"AND NOW, by the power vested in me by God and the state of Mississippi, I pronounce you husband and wife."

Brother Curtis Wimple beamed with pleasure as he looked from bride to groom. "You may kiss your bride, Kane."

Grinning broadly, Kane took Alex into his arms and planted a long, thorough kiss upon her trembling, though smiling lips. The many guests crowded into the church on this beautiful Saturday afternoon burst into applause to express their approval of Kane's choice of a mate.

The three ladies seated together in the front row dabbed at their eyes with lace-edged handkerchiefs.

"I told you she was the one," Dottie whispered to her sister, as the organ swelled into the music Alex had chosen to accompany them when she and Kane walked together down the aisle. "I told you she was perfect for him."

Mildred nodded agreement. "Yes, you were right," she murmured, watching as Alex and Kane swept past, both glowing with so much love and happiness, she couldn't help but smile in response. "And I'm glad. She'll make him a fine wife."

"Yes," Dottie agreed contentedly, smiling at Melanie, the maid of honor, who looked utterly beautiful in a red velvet gown so appropriate to the mid-December wedding. Even though Dottie hadn't thought Melanie right for her son, she liked the young woman very much and was pleased that Melanie had begun dating Kane's new partner, Dr. Stephen Lee. Everyone agreed that Melanie and Stephen seemed like an ideal couple.

"Alex was everything Kane wanted, Mildred," Dottie murmured, looking at her sister. "It doesn't matter whether she can cook or sew or anything else we could have demanded of her. All that matters is that she loves Kane and she makes him happy. That's all I ever wanted for him. For both my children," she added, beaming at her daughter, who sat nearby, a toddler in her arms and a loving husband at her side.

"They're very lucky."

Hearing the faintest trace of wistfulness in her sister's voice, Dottie reached out to take Mildred's hand into her own. "Yes, they're lucky young people. And we're lucky, too, Millie. We have each other."

Mildred's stern face softened into a smile. "I know, Dottie. I know."

"An entire week alone together," Alex said, shaking her head in exaggerated disbelief. "I can't believe it's really going to happen."

"Believe it," Kane advised her, glancing away from the road ahead and pulling one hand from the steering wheel to pat the breast pocket of his jacket. "I've got the airline tickets right here. And my pager is safely at home, tucked away in my sock drawer. It wouldn't work in Antigua, anyway," he added thoughtfully.

Alex giggled. "No, not even *your* pager has that much range. You're sure Stephen and Angie can handle everything while you're gone?" she asked. Kane's partner and a young woman resident from the Andersenville hospital would be lending a hand, while Kane was away on his honeymoon.

As much as she would have liked a longer wedding trip with him, Alex had agreed with Kane that a week was really all he could manage for now. Kane had promised to take vacations with her whenever he could, longer ones as the practice grew to the point where he could spare more time away.

"I'm sure the clinic will get along without me for seven days," Kane answered decisively. "This next week is all ours, Alex. Just the two of us."

"Maybe the three of us by the time we get back," she murmured, thinking of the possible consequences of seven, glorious nights in a tropical paradise. She and Kane had decided not to wait to start their family. They were both ready for parenthood, and, as Kane was so fond of saying, when it was right, it was right.

Alex knew that having a baby with Kane was exactly right for her.

She settled happily into the passenger seat, impatient for the honeymoon to begin. Idly she watched the passing scenery, remembering how she'd searched that same rural landscape for signs of civilization only a few months before, when she'd thought herself lost in the boonies. Now she couldn't imagine a more beautiful place to live and raise her children.

She giggled when they passed a fenced pasture, where a black-and-white cow munched contentedly on a tuft of hay as it watched their car pass. To her romance-dazed eyes, it had almost appeared as if the cow wore an expression of approval on seeing Alex and Kane together. If Alex hadn't known better, she would have sworn . . .

She laughed softly, shaking her head at her own foolishness.

"What's so funny?"

She turned to smile at her husband, deciding not to share the joke with him this time. He really was going to believe she had a thing about cows, if she wasn't careful! "Nothing. I'm just happy."

His smile made her heart turn over in her chest. "I'm glad," he murmured. "I plan to spend the rest of my life keeping you that way."

She sighed blissfully. *Wow*, she thought. It was almost like a fairy tale.

She could almost see the headline. Famous Author Lives Happily Ever After.

A Note from Gina Wilkins

"The Princess and the Pea" has been my favorite
fairy tale ever since I saw Carol Burnett's
television comedy version, "Once Upon a
Mattress." I was amused by the idea of a family
"testing" new candidates for inclusion in their
clan, and the lengths they'd go to in order to
make sure the match was "the right one." A real-
life marriage usually involves more than the bride
and groom—the young couple has to learn to
juggle the bride's family, the groom's family and
all the hopes, traditions and expectations of both
sides. It's not always easy, as many newlyweds
(and oldy-weds) can attest.

I was also intrigued with the concept that most
people seem to have a perfect mate out there
somewhere, even though that right match may
sometimes initially appear to be all wrong. Love
isn't always—or even usually—logical or
predictable. Sometimes it appears when least
expected, and between the least likely candidates.
That's what makes it so fascinating. I hope you
had as much fun reading my version of "The
Princess and the Pea" as I did writing it!

This month's
irresistible novels from

Temptation

WHEN IT'S RIGHT by Gina Wilkins
Live the fantasy...in Lovers and Legends

Once upon a time, a handsome prince wanted a wife, so he devised a test—or so the story goes. Alexandra Bennett was having a bad day. Her sports car had gone off the road and she turned up bedraggled and injured on the doorstep of Dr. Kane Lovell. He had the best bedside manner, but was she the right woman for him? He needed a lover *and* a wife—and she was only good at the loving part...

LOVE SLAVE by Mallory Rush

Being auctioned off in a white slave market was the most dangerous assignment of private detective Rachel Tinsdale's career. But perhaps her determined client, who had very personal reasons for wanting to infiltrate that dark business, was the true danger.

BEWITCHING by Carla Neggers

Hannah Marsh and Win Harling seemed like a perfect match. But things weren't to stay perfect for long. Their families had been feuding for three hundred years, so would they bury the hatchet in peace or into each other's skulls!

NOT MY BABY! by Judith McWilliams

When a young runaway landed on Marcy Handley's doorstep claiming to be her daughter, Marcy was confused. She was adamant about not being Stephanie's mother, but the girl's bachelor uncle saw that Marcy was working miracles with his niece. Why wouldn't Marcy tell him the truth?

FREE
GOLD PLATED BRACELET